THE QUEEN'S GAMBIT

JESSIE MIHALIK

COPYRIGHT

THE QUEEN'S GAMBIT
Copyright © 2018 by Jessie Mihalik
ISBN-13: 978-1721619672
ISBN-10: 1721619674

Excerpt from *Polaris Rising* copyright © by Jessie Mihalik

NYLA Publishing
121 W 27th St., Suite 1201, New York, NY 10001
http://www.nyliterary.com

DEDICATION

To Dustin, with love.
Let's get in a spaceship and
go have adventures.

ACKNOWLEDGMENTS

I'd like to thank the following people for their help and support.

Thanks to my agent, Sarah E. Younger, whose insightful feedback made this a far stronger story. Thank you to Natanya Wheeler for the cover design, and thanks to everyone at NYLA who helped bring the book into the world!

Thanks to Tracy Smith and Patrick Ferguson for reading chapters as I wrote them and offering feedback along the way. Thank you to Whitney Bates for getting me out of the house for some much needed coworking time. Thanks to Ilona and Gordon for all of the help and advice.

My deepest appreciation to the beta readers who generously volunteered their time and energy to improve the story: Regina Brandt, Alex Curran, Julie Ferm, Amanda Larson, and Liv W. You all are the best!

My love and gratitude to my husband, Dustin, who is my biggest supporter and greatest cheerleader. I love you so much.

Finally, thanks to all of the readers who followed along as the story was posted on my website, www.jessiemihalik.com. I am planning to continue the series in the late fall of 2018, and once again it will be posted first as a free serial.

1

I lowered my spaceship's cargo ramp and slipped into the night with the ease of long practice. The ship vanished as soon as I stepped away, hidden by the best stealth money could buy.

Darkness and I had always been friends, but something in the air tonight set my teeth on edge. After a few minutes, I stopped in the deep shadows cast by a partially collapsed wall and surveyed the building in front of me.

Twenty stories tall and one of the few structures still standing after years of war, the former office tower loomed like a shadowy monolith out of the sea of rubble surrounding it. My sense of unease grew.

The building looked as dark as a tomb. I would've expected at least a few lights, especially in the top floors. Had they blacked out all of the windows or was I operating on bad information?

Or perhaps the Quint Confederacy knew I was coming.

The Kos Empire and the Quint Confederacy had been locked in an intermittent territorial war for the last three decades. The fighting usually stayed at the intergalactic border between the disputed territories, but sometimes it spilled over to distant, unimportant planets like this one. Nowhere in the universe was entirely safe.

I had hoped that Valentin Kos, the newly crowned Kos Emperor, would end the war, but so far all he'd managed to do was get captured. At least his stupidity would feed my people for years, once I rescued him and then ransomed him back to the Kos Empire for a hefty fee.

I continued scanning the building while I waited. A few minutes later, a distinctive tickle in the back of my mind indicated an incoming neural link—my contact was right on time. I mentally activated the link and asked, *Jax, are you there?*

The mental response came across as a garbled burst of static then silence. I waited as patiently as I could—which wasn't very— to see if Jax could fix the link. A security specialist who had yet to find a system he couldn't crack, I needed his eyes on the building's video feeds or I'd be going in blind.

More static crackled across the link.

I took the extra time to do a final check of my equipment. I wore a stretchy black stealth suit that would help me slip past any perimeter security that Jax missed. My braided black hair disappeared in the dark and most of my light brown skin was hidden by the stealth suit. My uncovered face would be visible in low light, but it was a liability I had learned to mitigate because I hated camouflage paint.

Soft leather boots hugged my calves and protected my feet but kept my footsteps light. A belt around my waist secured a holstered electroshock pistol, an extra magazine of stun rounds, and a sheathed ceramic knife. I would've preferred more weapons, but tonight I traveled light in the name of stealth.

Adrenaline dripped through my veins. I used the familiar high to sharpen my focus and push away the anxiety I'd been feeling. I couldn't afford any mistakes tonight.

Then the top floor of the building lit up with plasma rifle fire.

Jax! Something is going on. Should I hold or go? I mentally asked across the link. More static responded. *Jackson Leopold Russell, get this link working and answer me right now or so help me...*

Sorry, sorry! There's no reason to bust out my full name, Samara Rani, he said irritably, emphasizing my name. His faint mental voice continued, *I'm here. Mostly. Our neural link is being jammed. Give me five minutes to get it sorted.*

I don't have five minutes, I said. *There's a shit-ton of plasma fire happening on the top floor and I'm already two minutes behind schedule. Do you have the vid feeds?*

Only of the outside, he said. *Your path to the building is clear. The inside feeds are proving tricky.*

Get eyes on the inside or kiss the rest of your contract money good-bye, I warned.

He grumbled but didn't reply.

I started toward the building, carefully working my way along the path Jax and I had planned. Cloud cover blocked the light from the moon and stars, forcing me to rely on the specialty contact lenses I wore. They automatically adjusted to the dark, enabling basic night-vision. I could see, but only in shades of greenish gray. I couldn't afford the ocular implants that would let me see in full color in the dark.

I couldn't afford many of the things that would make this job more doable and less crazy stupid.

I paused at the side door and took a deep breath. The easy part was over. If I went through this door, I was committed. No one knew I was here; I could leave and no one would be the wiser.

Except my people would still be starving.

Decision made, I gripped the door handle and pulled. The door didn't budge. *Jax! The side door is locked. Remind me why I'm paying you a mountain of credits for this?*

Because I'm the best, he said. I heard the lock click. *Try it now. You're clear to the elevator.*

I'm taking the stairs, I said.

Up twenty stories? Samara, you're crazy.

Maybe, I agreed. But an elevator was a trap waiting to happen, either en route or once it hit the top. At least with a stairwell I had more than one exit path.

You're clear to the stairs, Jax said. *I'm still trying to get the rest of the vid feeds. You'll be blind in the stairwell.*

I'll take my chances, I said.

The stairwell was as dark as the rest of the building. I cleared the stairs one floor at a time, moving as quickly as I dared. I didn't run into anyone else, but all of the doors I tried were locked. If I needed an escape, I'd either have to get Jax to unlock them or retreat all the way to the ground.

On the twentieth-floor landing, I paused. *Jax, I'm at the top. Do you have video?*

A burst of static blasted across my mind just as the building shook, rocked by an explosion I could feel but not see. *Jax, what the hell is going on in there?*

It's chaos, he said, his voice staticky. *It seems Kos soldiers are attempting to retrieve their emperor. And the Quint Confederacy mercenaries are resisting, naturally.*

I suppressed the urge to bang my head against the wall. Couldn't the Kos Empire have waited *one freaking day*? I needed that ransom money.

Jax continued, *But the Kos soldiers seem to have underestimated the Quint forces, again. They're getting their asses handed to them.*

Send me the vid feeds so I can see what I'm up against, I said.

No can do, I'm afraid. The whole area is actively jamming neural links. It's all I can do to keep our voice channel open.

I pinched the bridge of my nose and thought patient thoughts. It didn't help. *Follow my progress and let me know if I'm about to walk into a squad of soldiers. You are capable of that much at least, right?*

No need to get snippy, Sammy dear, Jax said in a saccharine tone guaranteed to enrage.

It worked. *It's Samara or Queen Rani to you. And this is not snippy. When I get snippy, people die*, I said.

4

Oh, so you're still pretending to be queen of that uncouth group of heathens you call subjects?

The Rogue Coalition took in anyone tired of the fighting between the Kos Empire and the Quint Confederacy. And while it was true we had a higher-than-usual number of people with less-than-legal professions, they were vastly outnumbered by the influx of refugees, mostly women and children, who'd lost everything during the war.

Still, no one got to insult us without repercussions.

The Rogue Coalition named me their Queen and so their Queen I remain. Insult them again and you'll get to see why they chose me. I let deadly promise sink into my voice. *It would be my pleasure to enlighten you. Personally.*

I hadn't set out to become Queen, but now that I was, I took my job seriously. My people had given me the power to decide their fate.

And the crushing responsibility to ensure their health and safety.

Jax's voice spluttered across the neural link. *Geez, it was a joke. Lighten up.*

It wasn't a joke, and it wasn't funny. Can we get back to business? I asked.

Neural links weren't always good about transmitting nonverbal communication but I caught his huff just fine. *Fine,* he grumbled. *The hall outside the stairwell is clear for the next thirty seconds.*

I pulled out my electroshock pistol and eased open the stairwell door. The hallway was lit with intermittent emergency lights that cast weird shadows in the smoke and dust swirling through the air. Visibility was shit, even with the help of my lenses. I turned right down the hall.

Samara, what are you doing? Jax shouted in my mind. *Go left. Left!*

I memorized the floor plan. Left is a dead end. Are you trying to get me killed?

Left was a dead end, but that was before the Kos soldiers blew a hole in it. If you keep going right, you're going to run into a squad of Quint mercenaries. He paused. *But, by all means, keep going. I have popcorn standing by.*

I changed direction and headed left. *Fine, left it is. Which room?*

First one on the right after the stairwell, Jax said. *Incoming!*

His warning came just after I'd already spotted the two soldiers ahead of me. I didn't have time to figure out which side they worked for and it really didn't matter—I needed to rescue Emperor Kos myself. I shot them both before they had time to draw their plasma pistols. The stun rounds sent them to the floor. They'd be out of commission for the next ten minutes at least.

Wow, nice shooting, Jax said.

I grunted in acknowledgment. *Any other surprises I should be aware of?*

Two more ahead. They'll detect you before you make the door.

Seriously, Jax? I asked. *Stun rounds don't grow on trees, you know. This was supposed to be a stealth mission. I'm not loaded for full combat.*

Suck it up, princess. You're the one that went charging in without waiting for information.

I sighed and crept down the hall. Two figures appeared through the haze. I shot them both and they slumped to the ground without a sound.

Did you just shoot them in the back? Jax asked. *That's hardly fair.*

Truth be told, I couldn't see them well enough to know which way they were facing. But their lack of reaction made more sense if they had been facing away. *I don't have time to play fair, and I wouldn't even if I did.*

I stepped over the soldiers' bodies. The door on the right stood open. Air currents pushed smoke and dust out into the hall.

That's your door, Jax said. *As far as I can tell, the room is clear, but some of the cameras are out.*

I eased into the room, sweeping for enemies. Chunks of debris littered the area. Dust and smoke swirled on the breeze coming through the gaping hole in the side of the building.

The Kos soldiers did this?

Yes, Jax said.

The explosion had also blasted a hole through the floor and part of the wall in the back of the room—Jax was right, this was no longer a dead end. The Kos soldiers must've expected to be long gone before the blast because it could've taken out the whole floor.

Where is the Emperor?

You want the good news or the bad news? Jax asked. I growled across the neural link and he continued, *Okay, okay. The good news is the Quint mercenaries stashed him close by.*

And the bad news? I asked, already dreading what he was going to say.

Well, the bad news is that the only path to him leads you right through the fire zone between the Quint mercs and the remaining Kos soldiers. How fast are you?

Many years ago, I had paid a small fortune for biological augments that made me stronger and faster, but even so, I wasn't *that* fast. *I can't dodge plasma pulses, Jax. And they won't be using stun rounds. Find a way around.*

There's nothing. He dropped into silence. *Wait, look down, is that a hole in the floor? Can you see the crawlspace?*

I peered into the hole. The blast had revealed a narrow utility crawlspace between this floor and the one below. *Yes, I can see it,* I said.

Do you have any breaching charges? he asked.

No. Stealth mission, remember?

You're killing me, he groaned. *No choice, you're going to have to go through the middle. It's a straight shot. I will unlock the door. It has a sensor, so it'll open as soon as you get close. I'll lock it behind you to give you time to free the Emperor and plan your escape.*

Seriously, that's your grand plan? Run for my life through an active fire zone?

If you have a better idea, I'm all ears. But based on what I'm seeing, you have about three minutes before the last of the Kos soldiers are wiped out and every Quint merc converges on the Emperor.

Shit. I couldn't take out a fortified contingent of Quint mercs on my best day, even if I was loaded for combat and had a guardian angel sitting on my shoulder. If they made it to the emperor before I did, I could kiss the ransom money goodbye.

How are we going to get out? Surprise only works once, I said.

His room connects out the back. I can unlock the doors all the way to the balcony, then lock them behind you to buy you some time.

Couldn't I get in that way?

You could, but you'd still have to go through the Quint mercs to get there, Jax said. *They have the other hallway completely blockaded and there's no cover. The smoke is mostly on this side of the building.*

I can't believe I'm actually considering this, I said. *How many soldiers are left?*

A couple dozen Quint and five Kos. Half of them are between you and the Emperor. I suggest you move fast.

I peeked through the hole in the wall. According to the floor plan, it should be a large open room. Red pulses from the plasma guns lit up in the distance but thanks to the weird light refraction through the smoke, I couldn't tell how far away the soldiers actually were.

Two meters to your right is the path through the room that leads straight to the door where the Emperor is held. The path is a lighter color than the rest of the floor. I think it's marble.

Where are the soldiers? I asked.

On the far side of the room. The Quint mercs are keeping the Kos soldiers pinned down away from the door. You'll only be in their field of fire for a few seconds.

If I was smart, I would retrace my steps and disappear into the night. But it had taken weeks to track the Emperor's location and

I didn't have the money to pay informants a second time. If I walked away, the Rogue Coalition would starve.

Fuck.

I ducked through the hole in the wall and found the path right where Jax said it would be. *Let me know when you've got the door unlocked,* I said.

It's ready when you are. I suggest you go sooner than later because another Kos soldier just fell.

I sprinted through the smoke, thinking invisible thoughts. Plasma pulses lit up in front of me but I didn't slow down. A door loomed out of the darkness, close enough that I thought I would hit it.

The door slid open just as I was bracing for impact. Momentum carried me into the room, and agony arced up my spine as stun rounds slammed into my body. My muscles seized; I hit the ground and slid.

A trap. I'd just run face-first into a fucking trap. I couldn't move my body, not even to speak, but the neural link still worked. *Jax, please explain why there are two squads of Quint mercenaries in the room that supposedly held the Emperor,* I said, my mental voice eerily calm.

Sorry, doll, he said. *They pay better than you do. Though, to be fair, Emperor Kos really is in there with you.*

When I get out of here, you're a dead man, Jackson Russell, I promised.

His laugh echoed across the link. *Good luck with that. Enjoy captivity, Queen Rani.*

He cut the link before I could respond.

2

Two Quint mercenaries picked me up by my upper arms. My body dangled uselessly between them, caught in the thrall of the stun rounds. I recovered faster than most, but it would still be too little, too late.

I attempted a neural link out, but without Jax's intervention, all of my attempts at long-distance links failed. Even my ship's signal flickered in and out, and it was hidden nearby. The only steady link options were a few people in the room, but no way was I initiating a link with an enemy soldier.

The soldiers dumped me in a chair. They cuffed my hands behind my back, then secured them to the chair. They also secured my ankles to the chair legs.

I looked far more delicate than I was, which tended to make people underestimate me, but the Quint mercs weren't taking any chances. Jax must have warned them about my augments.

That traitorous bastard was going to die slowly.

My head lolled on my neck and I left it hanging even as feeling crept back into my body. I needed every advantage I could get because I doubted the Quint mercs just wanted to share a nice cup of tea.

A man wearing fatigues and heavy boots stepped in front of me. He buried his fingers in the top of my braided hair and jerked my head up. He was older, grizzled, with reddish-brown hair graying at the temples. I didn't recognize him, but that didn't mean much. The Confederacy employed more people than I'd met in my lifetime.

"We meet at last, Samara Rani. The Rogue Queen—or is it the Scoundrel Queen?" he asked.

He seemed disappointed when I failed to rise to his baiting. I didn't mind being called the Scoundrel Queen. If others thought we were just a bunch of rogues and scoundrels, the Rogue Coalition became a less appealing target. And anything that made others think twice before attacking us was okay with me.

"Doesn't matter, I suppose," he continued. "You walked in here like a lamb to the slaughter. You should've seen your face." He laughed then leaned down to peer at me with a skeptical look. "Jax told us you were talented, but I'm not so sure. Maybe he wasn't talking about your intelligence, huh?"

I'd heard worse—much worse, delivered much more cleverly. I didn't bother with a reply. Eventually he'd get around to why they'd grabbed me and then we'd be getting somewhere.

"Commander Adams," a younger male voice said from somewhere behind me.

The man in front of me straightened with an impatient look. Now I had a name to go with his face. He didn't know it yet, but his ass was mine. I smothered my smile.

"Sorry to interrupt, sir," the young man continued, "but I thought you'd want to know the last of the Kos soldiers have fallen."

Commander Adams flicked his eyes over my shoulder. A vicious grin tugged on the corners of his mouth. "Your men are dead, Emperor," he said. "More lives you could've spared if only you'd cooperate."

"And let you enslave the rest of my people? I think not," a surprisingly sonorous voice responded.

Holy shit, Jax hadn't been lying—the Emperor really was in the room with me. I resisted the urge to crane my neck around and look for him.

The commander sneered then turned his attention back to me. "Now, where were we, my dear?" he asked.

It took all of my considerable willpower not to say something provoking. I had no doubt that this evening would end in violence, but there was no need to hasten it along quite yet.

"Tell me about the Rogue Coalition," Adams said, his hand still locked in my hair. When I didn't respond, he tightened his grip until pain blossomed across my scalp. "We can do this the easy way or the painful way. Me, I prefer the painful way."

His sneer made me itch to punch him. I wondered how fast his story would change if I freed myself. I very much doubted he would prefer the painful way if I was the one dishing it out—bullies didn't like it when the tables turned.

"Does threatening an innocent woman make you feel like a man?" Emperor Kos asked.

I briefly closed my eyes. While I appreciated the sentiment, I would've appreciated it more if he'd kept his mouth shut. An angry man was an unpredictable man, and I needed Commander Adams to stick to the script: press me for details, try a little physical persuasion, and, when that failed, lock me up somewhere to recover until the next session.

Commander Adams's grip tightened as he wrenched my head around. I could see Emperor Kos out of the corner of my eye. His dark hair was matted to his head and bruises shadowed a handsome face.

The Emperor had on a gray shirt and black pants, and he was secured to a chair of his own. Hopefully the Quint mercs had only inflicted superficial wounds or escaping would be more difficult.

Adams said, "This *innocent woman* is Queen Samara Rani of the

Rogue Coalition and a criminal in her own right. She's the very woman you yourself have a bounty on. Her pirates have stolen cargo from Quint and Kos ships for nearly a year. You should be happy someone finally caught her for you."

Emperor Kos opened his mouth to respond, so I took drastic measures. "If you two need some privacy while you measure your dicks, I'd be happy to step outside," I said.

Commander Adams jerked my head back and glared down at me. "Where is your ship?"

I gave him my most patronizing smile. "What ship?"

I saw the slap coming a kilometer away but couldn't do anything about it. Pain blazed through my cheek and scalp as the sudden movement pulled against the hand in my hair. Even left-handed, the Commander packed a wallop.

"Where are the rest of your soldiers?" Adams asked.

When I didn't respond, he hit me with a closed fist. I let the pain flow through me. I had his name; I had his face. I just had to endure until I could escape.

I mentally pulled back. When he hammered a fist into my stomach, it still hurt like a sonofabitch, but it was a distant pain.

I sighed in blissful relief when, a long while later, I slipped into the welcoming arms of unconsciousness.

I AWOKE to a cacophony of aches and pains. Commander Adams had worked me over, but he'd stopped short of inflicting debilitating damage.

My hands were still secured behind my back but now I was on my side on the floor. My left arm felt leaden, hopefully because I'd slept on it and not because my shoulder was dislocated or worse.

A soft sound nearby snapped me back to the situation at hand. I kept my eyes closed and feigned sleep. The air stirred as someone leaned over me. A hand touched my jaw and I struck, lunging up head first. My skull cracked against something hard and the person above me fell back with a deep groan.

I twisted around and kicked out with my bound legs. I hit something soft and the groan turned into a grunt of pain. Based on the timbre of the voice, it was likely a man, but all I could see were legs and feet outlined in greenish gray. We were in a pitch-black room but they hadn't taken my contact lenses. I pulled back for another kick.

"Queen Rani, stop, I'm not your enemy," the man snapped. He rolled away and sat up. "Your breathing changed. I was checking if you were awake. Clearly, you are."

A dark smear of blood ran from his nose. His face was bruised even more than before, but Emperor Kos was easy to recognize. Clean away the blood and bruises and the man would be gorgeous —the result of a millennia-long dynasty and the best genetics money and power could buy.

The Quint mercs had untied the Emperor's arms. His legs were still shackled. He held himself stiffly, but that could be because I'd just kicked him.

Emperor Kos watched me with wary suspicion, proving he could see. His eyes didn't glow with the telltale sheen of night-vision contact lenses, so he had some sort of augmentation, likely biological. People as rich as the Emperor didn't bother with mechanical ocular implants.

"How long have I been out?" I asked as I levered myself up into a sitting position. The mercs had taken my belt and weapons but left me in the stealth suit and boots.

"Two hours, maybe," he said. "Without being able to connect to the net, it's hard to tell."

I mentally reached for the net and came up empty. This room blocked all signals—I couldn't even see my ship. Without the constant background noise of an active net connection my mind seemed too quiet, too still.

I had trained to deal with the abrupt loss of connection and could also disconnect for particularly delicate jobs. But for normal people, forcibly cutting off their net connection amounted to psychological torture.

"How are you, Emperor Kos?" I asked. "Any injuries I should be aware of?" *Is the lack of a net connection making you crazy?*

"Please, call me Valentin. I only have minor injuries so far, though I think you might've cracked a rib. Why are you here?" he asked.

"I'm here for you," I said.

"My advisors hired the Rogue Queen to rescue me?" he asked skeptically.

"If you want something found in this universe, I can find it," I said, dodging the question. "And you might as well call me Samara. 'Queen Rani' makes me feel far fancier than I am and 'the Rogue Queen' is a mouthful."

"Did you lead my soldiers here to die?" he asked.

"No, they managed that bit of incompetence on their own. No one told me that Kos soldiers were attacking tonight. My mission was entirely separate."

Pins and needles stabbed my left arm as the blood flow resumed. First things first, I needed my hands in front of me. Thankfully, these cuffs had a spreader bar designed to keep my hands separated to make lock picking more difficult. It meant I could slide my arms under my butt rather than having to dislocate my shoulder to pull them over my head.

It took some ungraceful wiggling, but I managed to get my hands in front of me. Emperor Kos looked far more impressed than the move deserved.

A look at the cuffs proved what I'd suspected—they were an older style that many units still used because they were harder to pick. Of course, the cuffs had been around long enough that people who made a habit of getting put into them had also had plenty of time to practice getting *out* of them, myself included.

I needed to have a plan before I took them off or the Quint

soldiers would just slap me back in them. And a lot of that plan depended on how helpful—and useful—Emperor Kos would be.

"How long have you been here?" I asked. "Do they normally keep you in this cell?"

"I've been moved three times since they grabbed me. We've been here a little over a week. Last night was the second time I've been out of this room since we arrived."

The light mental tickle of a waiting neural link took me by surprise. I glanced sharply at Emperor Kos who nodded very slightly. My neural link connection was protected by the strongest defenses I could buy or build and wasn't open to unknown connections—he shouldn't have been able to contact me without permission.

In fact, he shouldn't even be able to *see* my link, much less connect to it.

I double-checked all of my mental firewalls, but I had a feeling that he was playing on an entirely different level. However, if we wanted any hope of escaping, neural link transmission was the best way to communicate secretly.

The link connected with an unusual burst of static. *I'm encrypting the signal,* Emperor Kos said through the link, *to prevent eavesdropping.*

Neural links were heavily encrypted by default, so he must be adding an additional layer of protection. The fact that he could— and thought that he needed to—made me question just how secure these links were in the first place.

The companies that handled the required brain implants guaranteed that their encryption was unbreakable. Now I wasn't so sure, even though Jax had never managed to break the encryption and he was the best hacker I knew.

You sound like Emperor Kos, but one can't be too careful. Touch your right eyebrow with your left pinky, I said.

He raised said eyebrow but followed my instructions. *Samara, I told you to call me Valentin,* he said.

I ignored the request. The intimacy of a first name made him *real,* made him a person and not just a payday. It was a complication I didn't need.

My head throbbed. I rubbed my forehead and used the movement to pull a pin from my hair and palm it. I had pins sewn into the seams of my stealth suit, but if the mercs were going to make it even easier, I wasn't going to complain.

I pulled my knees up and rested my forehead against them. The move was calculated to make me look small, harmless, and hopeless. It would also make it less apparent that we were linking.

I peeked at Emperor Kos. His frown smoothed out into a neutral expression when he caught me looking. So I wasn't the only one plotting. *How did you link without my permission?*

State secret, he said with a grin. Even bruised and with a busted lip, his grin hit me like a meteor. I sucked in a surprised breath as unexpected heat pooled low in my belly. *Can you get out of the cuffs?* he asked.

The question returned my attention to thoughts of escape. *Yes. How often do they check on you? Do you know anything about the guard rotations?*

They turn the lights on in the morning and someone brings me breakfast. Some days Commander Adams tries to get me to talk, but mostly it's just a random guard bringing food. Someone also brings me dinner. Other than that, the door doesn't open. The lights go out at night, and there is a camera in the corner.

I couldn't wait for the guards to open the door on schedule. They'd be expecting an escape attempt. Which meant I needed to provide them a reason to open the door early. Something urgent.

A plan began to form. It was risky, but everything was risky at this point. I let it simmer in my subconscious and started picking the lock on the left cuff. It was tricky with my arms wedged between my chest and legs, but it kept the cuff out of sight of the cameras. I returned to my questions.

"Any luck linking out while you've been here?" I asked aloud to keep the guards guessing.

Emperor Kos followed my lead. "I can't connect even when the door is open." He continued across the link, *I tried last night but although the block was lighter, I'm not sure the message got out.*

The mercenaries were being unusually careful with Emperor Kos. Most Quint mercs were hotheaded and impulsive, but this squad was a higher caliber. The Quint Confederacy wanted something from the Emperor. Badly. But what?

Whatever it was, they wanted him kept alive, which was ideal for me.

The handcuff unlocked. I left it around my wrist and carefully wrapped my arms around my legs until I could reach the lock on the leg shackle. The shackle was clamped to my ankle over the thin leather of my boots. I had to assume the guards were onto me at this point, so I moved quickly.

Do you have an escape plan? Kos asked.

Yes. It goes like this: step one, escape, I said. I didn't add that step two was ransom him and step three was profit—he'd find that out soon enough.

I hoped for something a little more concrete, he said. *I tried to over-power a guard and got this,* he pointed to his bruised face, *for my effort. I think they are augmented.*

I would be more surprised if the soldiers, especially the guards, *weren't* augmented. It wasn't an impossible situation, not quite, but it was far from ideal. We needed to escape tonight, while the mercs were still recovering from the Kos soldiers' attack. If we failed tonight it could take days or weeks to find another opening to escape, time I didn't have.

The leg shackled unlocked. *Showtime.* I let a good dose of crazy slip into my smile. Emperor Kos flinched back. "You thought I was here to *rescue* you," I said. "That's adorable."

He frowned. "But—"

I cut him off. "Your brother sends his regards," I said.

With that, I attacked.

3

I tackled the Emperor to the floor and pinned his arms with my knees. I clenched my hands around his neck and squeezed hard enough to block his airway. I hadn't warned him because I needed his reaction to be real. It took him a second, but once he realized he couldn't breathe, he began to fight in earnest.

What are you doing! he shouted at me across the neural link.

Keep fighting and don't pass out, I warned. I let off just enough for him to grab a desperate breath then retightened my fingers. He writhed under me, trying to buck me off, but what I lacked in mass, I made up for in strength. I kept him pinned.

The door lock clicked open. A guard entered pistol first, but I was already moving. He didn't expect my speed and his shot went wide.

I swung the heavy shackle still attached to my right arm and smashed it into his temple. As he fell, I grabbed his arm and turned the electroshock pistol on the guard behind him. She dropped like a rock, stunned.

Stun rounds meant they were trying to recapture us instead of kill us, which was a tiny bit of good news.

"Time to move, Emperor!" I yelled. He was still on the ground, gasping like a fish out of water. His legs were shackled and I didn't have time to pick the locks, so I squatted down and pulled him over my shoulders.

His frame dwarfed mine, but my augments made me far stronger than I looked. Augmented muscles and bones barely flinched at the added weight as I stood with the Emperor draped across my shoulders.

I picked up the second guard's plasma pistol and handed the Emperor the electroshock pistol. "Do you know how to use this?"

He nodded shakily.

"Shoot anything that moves," I said. "Do not hesitate. And for the love of all that's holy, don't shoot me."

I caught my ship's flickering signal and opened a connection. I could carry the Emperor for as long as I needed to, but we didn't have a lot of escape options. I directed my ship to remain cloaked but to maneuver closer. We'd have to risk a building-to-ship transfer because I very much doubted we'd be able to make the stairs.

I eased us out into the hall. A guard popped out from behind the nearest corner and I shot him on reflex. He went down in a cloud of red.

After two more turns, I knew where we were on the floor plan I'd studied. Our best chance of escape was from the balcony. We'd have to cross half the building to get to it, but it was still better than the three quarters of the building we'd have to cross to access the stairs.

Making a split-second decision I hoped I wouldn't regret, I backtracked one turn. The rest of the floor had gone silent, a sure sign that the mercs knew we'd escaped. "Can you eavesdrop on the soldiers' neural link?" I asked the Emperor. It should've been impossible, but someone who could see my link might be able to do the impossible.

"I'm not—"

"Yes or no?" I demanded.

"Yes," he said, his reluctance clear.

"Do it. Loop me in if you can. If not, let me know what they're up to."

It took a few seconds, but Commander Adams's voice filled my head, directing troops to various points around the floor. He was trying to surround us.

"They can't hear you," Kos said, "even if you transmit to me over the link. Your connection is receiving only."

I opened a door on our left and was met with a wave of plasma fire.

Rani is in here! a soldier called across the link.

Don't harm the Emperor! Commander Adams barked. He ordered two squads to converge on our location and another squad to cover the exits.

Time to move.

A peek around the door provided me with the soldier's position. I ducked back and a plasma pulse slammed into the wall across from the doorway. So much for not aiming for the Emperor.

I counted to three, then rounded the door and shot the soldier in the head—he hadn't moved. He went down with a look of surprise on his face.

I didn't have time to gloat. I moved across the room and out the door on the far side. The Emperor shot at someone with a muted curse.

Rani has the Emperor, a soldier reported.

Find them! Commander Adams ordered.

Listening to the soldiers' neural link, I avoided the squads heading our way and put some distance between us. With the exits blocked, we'd have to fight our way out. I needed the Emperor on his feet.

The next door I tried wouldn't open. I stepped back and

kicked it in. Emperor Kos grunted as I jostled him, but no one inside the room tried to kill us, so I chalked it up as a win.

Given a tiny reprieve, I set the Emperor down and started picking the lock on his right ankle shackle.

"Samara, my brother didn't send you to kill me, did he?" Emperor Kos asked.

"Of course not," I said. "But the fact that you believed he did says a lot about your family."

"Oh, there's no doubt he would if he thought he could get away with it. But I don't think you'd take the job."

The lock snapped open. I looked up and met his eyes. "Don't paint me with a halo or you'll be disappointed."

A Quint merc peeked into the room. The next time she appeared, I shot her. The Emperor spun in time to see her slump to the floor. He turned back with wide eyes.

I pointed at the shackle still locked around his left leg. "Don't trip on that, Emperor."

He frowned. "My name is Valentin."

It wasn't worth the time it would take to argue. "*Valentin*, don't trip on that and try to keep up."

The smile he gave me for using his name nearly stopped my heart. I blinked at him, then shook myself out of whatever spell he'd cast on me and refocused on the mission. Escape, money, food—these were the only things that mattered.

———

WITHOUT VALENTIN'S body draped over my shoulders, I had more freedom of movement, but it also made me twitchy because I didn't know exactly where he was. I found myself constantly looking over my shoulder to ensure he hadn't wandered off or decided to shoot me in the back.

When I nearly shot *him* because he got between me and a Quint mercenary, I planted his left hand on my right shoulder.

"Do not move this hand. You go where I go, duck when I duck, and turn when I turn. Otherwise I'm going to shoot you and all of this will be for nothing, understand?"

Valentin nodded.

We moved faster now that I didn't have to wonder where he was. The Quint mercenaries were beginning to catch on to the fact that we were somehow listening in on their neural link. Their chatter quieted as the soldiers moved to other forms of communication.

I'd taken us on a circuitous route to the balcony so we avoided the main squads. My ship was in position. We just had to clear one more hallway and we'd be home free. Unfortunately, Commander Adams had realized we weren't heading for the stairs and had redirected his troops.

And thanks to the radio silence, I had no idea how many mercs waited between us and the balcony.

I paused before entering the final hallway. I'd looted a second plasma pistol from a downed soldier, but that was the extent of my firepower. I'd kill for a grenade or seven, but so far, I hadn't found any. Maybe Commander Adams didn't trust his grunts with explosives.

"Why did we stop?" Valentin asked.

Because I don't enjoy getting shot. I hadn't meant to send the thought through the link, but by the way his mouth compressed, he'd caught it anyway. I needed to be more careful.

I crouched down and peeked around the corner. The hallway looked clear, but between us and the balcony there was a large room off to the right. The door was open. I couldn't see in at this angle, but I didn't need to. With my luck, it was packed with mercs.

The glass door leading to the balcony reflected the brightly lit hallway and obscured whatever lurked outside. If Commander Adams had managed to get here first, we'd be running blind into an ambush. But with our options dwindling, I had to risk it.

I sighed. I *really* did not want to get shot.

"We're going to run for it," I said. I clamped my left hand around Valentin's right wrist. It meant I lost a gun, but I didn't trust him to follow my lead.

"I can't shoot left-handed," he said.

"Do your best, even wild shots will help, but speed is most important. Whatever happens, *do not slow down*. Ready?"

I didn't give him time to answer, I just pulled him into a run. Two meters before the open door to the room on the right, the world lit up with plasma fire.

I did not slow down. A pulse clipped my right shoulder but adrenaline blocked the pain. I shot the soldier responsible through the slice of the door I could see. He went down in a burst of pulses that gave me a tiny opening as the other mercenaries dove for cover.

I pulled Valentin into a sprint past the door. He jerked against my grip but didn't go down. Hopefully he'd only been grazed or this escape was about to get even more dicey.

The glass door to the balcony loomed in front of me. I waited until the very last second to shoot the glass. I exploded through the door, covered in shattered safety glass. Valentin came through behind me, still tethered by my grip on his wrist.

I had the brief satisfaction of seeing Commander Adams's surprised expression before I realized just how many mercenaries crowded the balcony. At least a dozen men and women stood in a loose semi-circle facing the door. They all had plasma weapons trained on us.

Time slowed as training and instinct took over. I wasn't going down without a fight, futile though it may be. And luckily for me, Commander Adams stood directly between me and freedom. Shooting him would be no hardship. I squeezed the trigger just as he shouted, "Fire!"

Three things happened at once.

Down! roared across the mercenaries' neural link, accompanied by a blast of mind-piercing sound. The mercs dropped like marionettes with cut strings. Several released their weapons to clutch their heads and the rest looked dazed. Only a few managed to get off shots and all went wide.

My own shot sailed over Commander Adams's head. I couldn't remember the last time I'd missed a shot, but with the echo of the neural link noise still ringing in my mind, I failed to compensate for his fall.

Valentin staggered and went down. His weight dragged me to a stop. One look and I knew where the mystery shout had come from—he looked like hell. Fresh blood trickled from his nose and white pain lines bracketed his mouth, clearly visible even with the limited night-vision ability of my contacts.

He'd bought us some dearly needed time, but it had cost him.

"Up, now!" I shouted at him. I pulled him up and dragged him into a stumbling jog. I shot the opposing soldiers as fast as I could squeeze the trigger, aiming for the ones recovering first.

The plasma pistol clicked empty. I threw it at the nearest soldier, then we were across their line. The balcony's edge was less than two meters away. I pulled Valentin forward, half carrying him.

The railing that would normally protect us from a fall was lowered to allow air taxis and ships to pick up passengers. The balcony extended beyond the side of the building. Below was nothing but twenty stories of dark, empty air.

Star-bright pain blossomed in my right thigh and my knee buckled. I gritted my teeth and threw myself toward the balcony's edge.

Valentin balked, but my grip did not loosen. Momentum pulled me over the edge and my iron grip on Emperor Kos yanked him right behind me.

Together we fell into the open air.

4

For one weightless, terrifying moment I thought I'd miscalculated the jump. Then we passed through *Invictia's* stealth field and the ship flickered into existence below us. In an impressively acrobatic move, Valentin jerked me close and used the momentum to spin himself beneath me.

I landed on him hard enough to hurt. I drew a gasping breath and pushed myself up, only to realize I was straddling him. I froze.

He grinned at me and not even the blood and bruises could disguise the interest in his gaze. Then he ruined the effect by bursting into a fit of coughing.

Shouts from above pulled my attention away from the man under me. "We're going to move, so don't freak out," I said. I used my mental connection to the ship to direct it away from the building and bring up the shields. The soldiers shouldn't be able to see us, and even if they could, the shields should protect us, but there was no reason to risk it.

The ship slid sideways as Valentin finally caught his breath. "We're not dead," he said.

"Not quite," I said. I tried to ignore how good his body felt under mine. He was big and solid and warm and I needed to move before my brain took a vacation. I started to climb off him, but he gently stopped me.

"You knew the ship was here," he said. "You should've told me. I thought you fell."

I raised a brow at him. "Somehow I doubt you would've jumped into the open air on my word alone. Also, I'm not sure you want to get into a discussion of who should've told who what," I said. "Because I seem to remember a certain someone taking out a dozen Quint mercs without lifting a finger."

His mouth tightened but he didn't reply. He touched my right thigh, whether to help me up or hold me in place, I'd never know, because he jerked his hand away. A dark smear covered his palm in my night-vision sight.

"You're bleeding," he said.

As if the reminder was all my body needed, pain blasted through the adrenaline fog. I swayed but covered it by rolling off Valentin. I pushed my abused body into a standing position. My leg wavered but held. I had about five more minutes without medical aid before I'd be down for the count.

"Let's get inside," I said. "There's an airlock in the middle." I pulled the Emperor to his feet and directed *Invictia* to open the hatch. I also directed the ship to shut down all outbound communication and block outgoing signals. I didn't need Valentin calling for help just yet.

The airlock was a tight fit for the two of us, and I ended up practically in Valentin's lap. This was the secondary airlock, only used in case of emergency. It wasn't designed to be a main entrance.

My thigh blazed with white-hot pain at every movement, but eventually the airlock released us and we climbed down into the wide main hallway that ran from the bridge to the cargo area. Luckily, medical was nearby—and so was everything else.

Invictia was a tiny ship, one of the smallest capable of faster

27

than light tunneling between galaxies. The bridge took up the front quarter of the main level. The middle two quarters housed the living areas. The captain's quarters, the tiny crew bunk, and the crew head were on the starboard side. Medical, the galley, and the small rec room I'd modified into three holding cells shared the port side.

The aft quarter of the ship included a compact cargo bay on the main level and the stardrive, auxiliary engines, and primary maintenance area on the lower level. Other maintenance crawl spaces snaked throughout the ship.

I ushered Valentin into medical without giving him a chance to poke around. "Were you shot?" I asked. I bent over to pick the lock on the shackle still clamped to my left leg and black spots danced in my vision. I'd lost more blood than I thought.

"Just grazes," he said. "You're in far worse shape. What can I do to help?"

The shackle unlocked. I removed my boots and then started peeling myself out of the stealth suit. The stretchy material fought me every step of the way. "Trauma shears are in the drawer over there," I said, pointing to the far wall. "Cut me out of this so I can dress my wounds."

Valentin moved across the room with relative ease. Whatever he had done earlier had knocked him down but hadn't done lasting harm.

Invictia was too small to have a proper medical diagnostic chamber and auto-doc. I'd have to make do with the handheld scanner and good old-fashioned triage until I got back to Arx, the Rogue Coalition's headquarters on Trigon Three.

Valentin cut my stealth suit away until I stood in only my boy shorts and sports bra. My right side was coated in blood from my shoulder to my calf. Mostly I'd been grazed but the bastard who'd hit my thigh had gotten off a solid shot.

"How are you still standing?" Valentin asked.

"Practice," I said, only half joking.

The plasma pulse had passed through my outer thigh and must've just missed the bone. A couple of centimeters to the left and we likely would not have escaped.

The medical scanner recommended a round in a med chamber, but since that wasn't an option, I went with the secondary recommendation—cleaning and bandaging. The injury, for all it hurt like a bitch, wasn't fatal, and the pulse had missed all of the major blood vessels.

I cleaned the wound, slathered it in renewal gel, then slapped on an elastomer bandage designed to mimic skin. Just to be safe, I also gave myself an injection of an immune booster and painkiller.

As the languid warmth of the painkiller spread outward from my thigh, I directed *Invictia* to take us off-planet. We needed to escape before the Quint Confederacy could send more mercenaries our way.

———

THE PAINKILLER KNOCKED off the worst of my pain, but it also muted the adrenaline that had kept me going. The world went distant and fuzzy. My fingers turned clumsy and I struggled to reach the wound on my shoulder.

"Hold still and let me do it," Valentin groused. I paused. I wasn't used to relying on other people, but perhaps he was right.

With my hesitation, Valentin took over. His hands trembled as his own adrenaline wore off. He hid it well, but the close call had shaken him deeply. Near-death experiences tended to have that effect on people, but he was holding up better than I expected.

He frowned in concentration as he cleaned and bandaged my shoulder and other wounds. He treated me gently. Drifting deep in the painkiller haze, something very much like affection bloomed in my chest.

"All done," he said a few minutes later. He looked me over. "You're smiling. Does that mean you're going to live?"

I met his eyes and again felt a jolt of desire. Maybe for one brief moment I could put aside the crushing weight of responsibility and just be a woman standing in front of an attractive man, celebrating the fact that we both were still alive.

"I'm fantastic," I said. I buried my hand in the short, dark hair at the back of his head and pulled him toward me. His eyes were gray and wide with surprise. A tiny bit of doubt reared its head, and I stopped with a breath of space between us. Had I read him wrong?

He hesitated for an eternal second and then groaned low and pulled away. My hand hovered in the air for a moment before I remembered to drop it. Valentin started to reach for me but stopped the motion halfway. He ran his hands through his hair in frustration.

"I'm sorry. I can't. You're high on painkillers. You rescued me. I won't repay that debt by taking advantage of you now." He muttered something else, but my pride was too busy trying to recover to catch it.

Heat climbed my cheeks as the rejection finally sank in. Embarrassment burned away the pleasant haziness until I was left with only cold reason.

And reason said I was a fucking idiot.

I *wasn't* just a woman, not anymore. I was a Queen with a plan —a plan thousands of people were counting on—and affection had no place in that plan. Kissing *definitely* had no place. Emperor Kos was a means to an end, and if I lost sight of that, I ran the risk of losing everything.

Commander Adams hadn't been wrong, either—the Kos Empire *did* have a bounty on my head. If I wasn't careful, I'd end up the one captured. I needed to stick to the script and get my head in the game.

I closed my eyes, took a deep breath, and tried to herd my

thoughts into some semblance of order. I pasted on a too-bright smile and met Valentin's gaze. "Sorry about that," I said. "I didn't expect the painkiller to affect me so strongly, but that's no excuse. I apologize."

"Samara—" Valentin started.

"Let's get you patched up," I said. "Where were you hit?"

He started to argue further but changed his mind after a glance at my face. "A pulse grazed my back," he said. "But I don't think it's too bad. It can wait."

I motioned him around with a little twirl of my fingers. He grumbled but turned around. His shirt gaped open from his shoulder blades. The pulse had burned through the fabric and just grazed his warm golden skin, leaving behind a long, narrow burn.

"Take off your shirt. It's trash, anyway. I'll find you a spare," I said. "The wound is shallow, but I'll put some renewal gel on it to speed up the healing."

Valentin pulled the shirt over his head revealing a surprisingly muscled back and sculpted arms. He might have genetics on his side, but he'd worked hard to build this much muscle. The real question was how—and why.

He half-turned, trying to see the wound over his shoulder. I caught a glimpse of a smoothly muscled chest before I forced my eyes away. The man was gorgeous. I didn't need any more mental images of his body haunting my dreams.

I focused and carefully dabbed renewal gel on the wound and then covered it with an elastomer bandage. It wasn't deep, but sometimes shallow plasma wounds stung worse than their deeper counterparts.

"Do you want a painkiller or just an immune boost?" I asked, already preparing the injector.

"I don't need either," he said. He turned to face me.

I frowned at him. "That wasn't an option. Painkiller, yes or no?"

"No, thank you," he said. "And I'm augmented to improve heal-ing, so you might as well save the immune booster, too."

"I'm not risking you getting an infection when the ship has such limited medical facilities. Give me your arm."

"I'm not going to die of infection in a few hours," he said with a smile, but he gave me his arm.

I pressed the injector against the skin of his upper arm—and hesitated. I met his eyes. He was still smiling, his expression warm, like he was trying to soften the blow of rejection.

Valentin wasn't what I expected, but that didn't change anything, not really. I pulled the trigger with a sigh and blamed the flash of regret on the painkiller still swirling through my system.

He stopped me before I could turn away. "Are you okay?" he asked.

"I will be," I said. Still, I couldn't quite shake my melancholy mood. "Do you ever wish you were someone else?"

His expression turned wistful. "When I was little, I'd sneak out of the palace to play with the boys in the city. It gave my nurses heart attacks, but those kids didn't care who I was, they just knew I was ready and willing to join the fray."

He paused, then continued, "I wasn't raised to be the Emperor; my life took a different path. But then Father secretly changed the line of succession two months before he died. He didn't ask me, didn't offer any explanation—hell, he didn't even tell me. My older brother Nikolas thinks I stole his crown. He refuses to talk to me and as you suspected, would likely prefer me dead."

Everyone knew about the last-minute succession change, but everyone assumed that Valentin *had* stolen the crown from his brother. If he truly hadn't, then it cast a whole new light on the past eleven months.

Valentin would've had to work fast to build support in a hostile house because no doubt his brother had been collecting allies and making deals since he was a child. And none of his brother's allies would be happy with Emperor *Valentin* Kos.

The fact that he had kept the crown—and his head—meant Valentin was far more cunning and determined than his recent actions had led me to believe.

Valentin's gaze dropped to the scar on my left collarbone. A plasma pulse had shattered the bone. I'd spent five days in hell before an auto-doc patched me up. I could've paid to have the scar removed, but I kept it as a reminder to not fuck up.

A reminder I dearly needed right now.

Valentin blinked slowly. "What about you, Samara, do you—" He shook his head and clutched at the wall behind him as he staggered backward a step. He leaned back against the wall, then slowly crumpled to the floor. He looked up in confusion.

"What's happening?" he asked, his voice slurred.

"It's just a little sedative. You'll take a nice nap while I get us out of here."

The confusion gave way to such a look of sheer betrayal that my heart twisted. Anger clouded his features as he slumped sideways. He glared at me from the floor.

"I... trusted... you," he ground out.

Sadness crept through me. "I know," I said softly. "Sleep well."

5

I left Valentin sleeping in medical and went to find him a shirt from the crew bunk. With his augments, I wasn't exactly sure how long he'd stay out. It might be as little as fifteen minutes, so the faster I got him into a cell, the better.

It was more difficult than I expected to wrestle his limp body into a shirt, but I finally managed it. With him fully dressed again, I picked him up and carried him two doors down. Pain stabbed down my right leg with each step but the bandage held.

I put Valentin in the cell across from the door and turned on signal isolation to prevent him from linking outside of the cell. After a moment's hesitation, I picked the lock on his remaining leg shackle and removed it. He'd be more comfortable without it.

With Valentin contained, I headed to the bridge. We had cleared the planet's atmosphere. And as far as the sensors were concerned, no one had followed us. If someone *had* followed us, their stealth system was better than mine. In a few more minutes we could make our first tunnel transit and hopefully lose any tagalongs.

"*Invictia,* close all neural link connections. Accept only my spoken commands and authenticated terminal commands until further notice."

My mental connection to the ship disappeared. "All neural connections have been closed," the ship said over the bridge loud-speakers.

I severed my connection to the net and closed all of the neural link sockets that listened for incoming connections. It might be overkill, but without knowing exactly how Emperor Kos's neural ability worked, I couldn't be sure.

At the thought of the Emperor, my mind drifted back to our almost kiss. I touched my lips. The painkiller had loosened its grip and I still wanted him. He affected me more strongly than anyone I'd met in a long, long time.

But he could have anyone he wanted, and while I was self-aware enough to know I was attractive in my own way, I was far from the stunning women he was likely used to at court.

I scowled. Jealousy wasn't a good look, especially not when the target was so far out of reach he might as well be a distant star in the night sky. I needed to keep my eye on the prize and get over the fact that he was the rare combination of smart, surprisingly kind, and damn attractive.

To keep myself busy, I plotted the course to the Rogue Coalition's headquarters on Trigon Three. The direct route required two tunnel transits. The stardrive needed a four-hour recharge before the second transit, but even so, I could be home in time for brunch.

However, I also needed to let the Kos Empire know that I had Valentin. Right now, we were in the middle of Quint space and communication was restricted, so if I wanted Kos to get the message sometime this century, I needed to be closer to a large communication hub.

I could hit the nearest hub in a single tunnel transit but it was still in Quint Confederacy space. I needed something in disputed space and the only nearby option was two tunnels away: Caldwell Prime 57.

Once a tiny frontier space station, Caldwell Prime 57 had grown to epic proportions. Rumor had it that seventy-five percent of the universe's black-market goods moved through CP57. Both Quint and Kos were desperate to control it, but CP57 had grown tired of the constant fighting and declared themselves independent—and they had the money, power, and numbers to back it up.

I plotted the course. Stopping by CP57 meant adding an extra tunnel transit—and another four-hour recharge—but it was safer than hanging around in Quint space. It also put me closer to Trigon Three if things went south. Decision made, I locked in the route. We would complete our first transit in ten minutes.

With the course set, I decided a shower was the next highest priority. The door to my quarters slid open, revealing painted walls of pale gold that reminded me of sunlight on a summer's day.

A large bed dominated the room. Because of the bed, I didn't have space for the typical sitting room, but I had managed to squeeze in a comfy overstuffed chair and a footrest. I rarely had company; I didn't need a second chair.

Designed and decorated for me alone, this room had been my haven for far longer than I'd been *Queen* Samara Rani.

I dug through the wardrobe looking for clothes that would be easy to put on with a busted-up shoulder and thigh. I decided on loose utility pants and a button-up shirt.

My tiny private bathroom had a sink, shower, and toilet. The mirror above the sink did not reflect a flattering picture. Dark circles shadowed the skin under my eyes and my right eye was ringed in black—Commander Adams had hit harder than I thought. And thanks to the blood loss, my light brown skin had taken on a sickly pallor. I looked like a dark-eyed, dark-haired wraith.

I stripped out of my underthings and stepped into the shower to let the water wash away the remnants of our escape. Bloody rivulets ran down my arms and legs.

Lulled by the warm water, I lost track of time, but the unmistakable vibration of the stardrive kicking in broke me from the daze. I washed my hair and then carefully washed around the bandages.

By the time I was done, my thigh throbbed in time with my pulse, a deep, stabbing pain that the painkiller couldn't completely alleviate. And after my last experience in humiliation, I wasn't eager to give myself another dose.

———

CLEAN AND DRESSED, I headed across the hall to the galley to find something to eat. The thought of food made me vaguely nauseous, but I at least needed to drink some juice to make up for the blood loss.

"Samara!" Valentin shouted. "Samara Rani, I know you can hear me. Let me out of here!" He banged something against the wall of his cell. "Samara!"

In the galley, I grabbed two energy bars and two bottles of rehydration fluid—I wasn't wasting apple juice on Emperor Kos. With no reason to delay further, I went to face the dragon.

Valentin stopped shouting when I entered the room. He stood close to the wall of his cell, and with all of his anger and annoyance focused on me, I was very glad we were separated by five centimeters of clear thermoplastic.

"I trusted you and you lied to me," he said without preamble.

"I didn't lie," I said. I pushed the bottle and energy bar through the narrow opening designed for food trays. Valentin ignored both items.

"You let me believe you were rescuing me," he bit out. "A lie by omission is still a lie."

"I *did* rescue you," I said. "You're safe. I won't torture you. I don't care what the Quint Confederacy wanted from you. As soon as your advisors pay me for my trouble, I'll deliver you directly into their loving embrace."

His eyes widened. "You're *ransoming* me?" he asked.

"Yes. How much do you think you're worth to your Empire? I was thinking ten million credits."

He shook his head. "I can't believe the rumors about you are true after all."

My own temper ignited. "Which rumors?" I asked. "The ones about how your stupid fucking war is sending thousands and thousands of refugees into neutral territories like mine, territories that can't feed the people they already have because that same war closed borders and shut down trade? Because that isn't rumor, that's *fact*."

Some emotion I couldn't name passed over Valentin's face before being replaced by a sneer. "No, I was the referring to the rumors that you're greedy and heartless."

I laughed. "Oh, I'm far worse than that. I will do whatever it takes to keep my people safe. You had better hope your advisors pay up quickly, Emperor Kos."

"They won't give you a single credit," he said with calm certainty.

"Then you'd better get used to that cell because you're going to be enjoying it for a long, long time."

He slammed his palm against the wall separating us. "Dammit, let me out of here. We can work something out."

"No," I said. "If you really want out, then start thinking of a way to get your advisors to pay your ransom faster—or pay it yourself."

"I don't want to hurt you," he said with cool menace, "but I will if I have to. I don't have time for this."

"You do what you have to do. But know this: if you do manage to hurt me, I'll leave you to the same fate my people are currently suffering. And starving to death is a terrible way to die."

"You can drop the act," he said coldly. His rage was being replaced with cool calculation, piece by piece. "We both know the people of the Rogue Coalition are fine. Playing for my sympathy won't save you."

I blinked at him, momentarily thrown. "Just to be clear," I said slowly, "you think my people aren't starving and that I risked my life to rescue you from Quint's clutches because…" I trailed off, interested to see how he'd finish that sentence.

"I *thought* you did it because the Kos Empire had hired you to. That was obviously wrong. Now, I think you did it to prove you could," Valentin said. "You saw an opportunity to further line your coffers and you took it."

"Wow." I shook my head in disbelief. "Wow," I said again. "Okay, here's a free piece of advice: fire your intelligence advisors. They're incompetent or they want you to look incompetent. Either way, you'd be better off without them."

Valentin narrowed his eyes and said nothing.

I opened my bottle of rehydration fluid and drank half of it. It tasted like I imagined sweaty old socks would taste, but I forced it down. I also nibbled on my energy bar while I let my temper settle.

Advisors were vitally important for a ruler, a lesson I'd had to learn after running myself ragged trying to stay on top of every issue. And the entire Rogue Coalition was just a few hundred thousand people on five planets—the Kos Empire spanned half of the known universe.

By design, advisors had an enormous amount influence. By filtering the data they passed on, they could shape an issue however they wanted. A few advisors working together could do a lot to undermine an unwanted leader, especially one whose attentions were occupied elsewhere.

Finally, I asked, "Did you replace the imperial advisors when you took over as Emperor?" If he truly hadn't stolen the crown, then the likely answer was no. He'd need the old advisors to keep some semblance of stability.

Valentin stared down his nose at me, every centimeter the forbidding, untouchable Emperor. "I don't see how that's any of your business," he said coldly.

"I don't know what your advisors are telling you," I said, "but if they are lying about the Rogue Coalition, they are likely lying about other things. You need to clean house. And maybe check a news outlet or two."

"Of course I check the news," he said, expression closed and calculating.

I rubbed my face. "Then dig deeper when you get home. Don't just swallow whatever your advisors are telling you. I thought you were incompetent or indifferent, but now I'm not so sure. I think your advisors are sabotaging you."

"I assure you that I am neither incompetent nor indifferent," Valentin said with a finality that signaled the end of the conversation.

I blew out a breath. It wasn't my problem, but I couldn't let it go without one more attempt. Despite everything, I actually *liked* him.

"Just do some independent research," I said. "Your people deserve that much from their Emperor."

His mouth flattened into a hard line.

"I've blocked all outgoing communication and shut down all neural link connections," I said, "so if you need me, you'll have to shout. Abuse the privilege and I'll turn on the soundproofing in your cell. We have four hours until our next tunnel. I suggest you sleep."

"If you let me go right now, I give you my word that I won't declare war on you, Queen Rani," Valentin said.

"You won't declare war anyway because it's going to be part of the ransom agreement. Believe it or not, I'm not stupid."

"I never said you were stupid," he said.

"No, just heartless and greedy. And you're about to get a first-hand look at just how much of both I am. I hope some of your advisors are smarter than you," I said as I turned to leave. "At least the ones who don't want you declared incompetent."

"Dammit, Samara, let me out," Valentin demanded.

I stopped in the doorway. "*Invictia,* turn on soundproofing in the cells," I said.

A chime sounded and Valentin's mouth moved but no words reached me. "I can't hear you," I said, "so feel free to shout yourself hoarse. I'll be back to check on you in a few hours."

The soundproofing was one-way, so Valentin could hear me just fine. He paused and then slapped his hand against the cell wall. He very clearly enunciated, "Fuck. You."

I looked him up and down. "While I appreciate the offer, I'm going to have to pass. That ship has sailed. You'll just have to use your imagination," I said with a wink.

His thunderstruck expression made me smile all the way out the door.

6

S afely back in my own quarters, I told *Invictia* to turn on monitoring in Valentin's cell. It would alert me to any irregularities, including if his vitals dangerously spiked or dipped. I had waited until I was alone because I didn't want to give him any ideas about how to get my attention. But I also didn't want him to die just because he couldn't call for help.

I drank the rest of my rehydration fluid and choked down the energy bar. Without a neural connection, I had to use the terminal embedded into the wall to check on the ship's systems. I'd forgotten how much trouble it was. All the sensors came back normal and no other ships were in range. Our flight was on schedule and proceeding as planned.

With a little more than three and a half hours to go until our next tunnel transit, I decided to take my own advice and get some sleep. I flopped into the bed and sighed in relief as some of the pressure on my thigh eased. The renewal gel greatly accelerated healing, but it would be a painful few days. I'd probably have to take another dose of painkiller when I woke up. I'd just stay far away from Valentin and everything would be fine.

"*Invictia*, set threat level four," I said. "And wake me up for any contact."

"Yes, Captain," the ship responded.

Threat level four was the highest level. At this level, the ship would sound an alert for anything it considered an anomaly, including if another ship moved within sensor range, even if the ship was flagged as medical or merchant. This far out into dead space, the chance of randomly running into another ship was miniscule.

Aware that the ship was far better at spotting threats than I would be, I lowered the lights. Fatigue dragged at me and I easily slid into sleep.

———

I SNAPPED awake to blaring alarms and flashing lights. I sat up and instinctively reached for my mental connection to the ship, only to come up empty. It took precious seconds to remember that I'd shut down all neural connections.

"*Invictia*, report," I said. "And silence the damn alarm."

"Unknown ship within sensor range," the ship responded.

"Show me." I checked the time. I'd slept for three hours. We still had half an hour until we could tunnel again.

The screen embedded in the wall lit up with an enhanced view from outside the ship. My stomach dropped at the sight. The real ship was lost in the vast darkness of space, but *Invictia* projected a model based on the sensor data. A large destroyer loomed well within attack range.

The stats streaming on one side of the display showed the ship was not broadcasting an allegiance. And they weren't running cloaked—they wanted me to know how outgunned I was.

So they weren't here to chat.

"*Invictia*, turn off soundproofing in the cells," I said as I ran in that direction. A second later, I heard Valentin s shouts.

"Did you call a destroyer?" I asked as soon as I cleared the door.

"What?"

"Did you get a message out? Is that your destroyer outside?"

"What? No. I don't think so," he said. "Is it flagged Kos?"

"No flag," I said.

"Then it's not mine. Are you sure it's here for us?"

"Oh, I'm sure," I said. "Hold on to something, it's about to get bumpy."

"Let me out! I can help!"

I ignored him and ran for the bridge. I dropped into the captain's chair and immediately started a system scan. Tunnel endpoints were not broadcast and this was not a busy hub—we were in deep space. The odds that a destroyer randomly tunneled to our exact location were so infinitesimal that it might as well be called impossible.

Someone had tracked my ship.

I only knew one slimy little bastard with the skills and opportunity to slip a tracker into my systems—Jackson Russell, my soon-to-be-dead former security specialist. I'd consulted with him for years, and once paid, he'd always stayed bought. Until now.

Two weeks ago, I'd bailed him out of a tight spot and given him a lift in return for new information on Valentin's location. I should've known better than to let him on my ship.

While the scan ran, I pulled up the enhanced feeds from the outside cameras and put them on the main screens lining the front of the bridge. The walls seemed to disappear as I stared out into the inky blackness of space.

The computer's depiction of the destroyer was tiny without the help of a long-distance zoom, but the fact that I could see it at all proved just how close they were. The actual ship twinkled through the computer overlay as their signal light flashed the pattern that indicated they were attempting to hail me.

Invictia's stealth systems were second to none, but destroyers were designed to hunt and kill hidden ships. If they didn't know exactly where we were already, then it was only a matter of time —most likely a very short time—before they did.

I debated the pros and cons of bringing up external communication and finally decided I didn't lose anything by listening to their demands. And it might buy me some time. If I pushed it, *Invictia* could tunnel again in twenty minutes. Until then, we were sitting ducks.

They must've been continuously signaling because the connection came through as soon as the communication array went online. I accepted and Commander Adams's grizzled face appeared on screen.

Son. Of. A. Bitch.

I hid my fury behind a lazy smile. "Commander, what a surprise. Have you also come to enjoy the solitude of deep space?"

"Surrender yourself and Emperor Kos, or we'll shoot you down," he said.

"You're too late. I've already dumped Emperor Kos," I said. "So you came all this way just for me. I'm flattered."

"Our sensors show two people aboard your ship, so forgive me if I don't believe you."

"You didn't seriously think I broke into an enemy building by myself, did you?" I scoffed with a laugh. Now that I'd been caught, I needed to shift blame away from the Rogue Coalition.

Luckily, I had the perfect scapegoat.

"The Kos Empire paid me a fortune to rescue Emperor Kos. They had a team waiting for him. I sent them on while my bodyguard and I stayed behind to play decoy. Ta da!" I said with a flourish.

Commander Adams remained skeptical, but I didn't care. I'd planted the seeds of doubt, and now I just needed to keep him from shooting at us until we were ready to tunnel. *Invictia* was a hell of a ship, but she was no match for a destroyer.

"Surrender peacefully or die," Adams said.

"Are you authorized to negotiate terms on behalf of the Quint Confederacy?"

"There are no terms to negotiate."

"So that's a no, I guess," I said. "Stop wasting my time and contact me again when you have someone authorized."

I closed the link.

My system scan came back with a whole lot of nothing. Whatever Jax had done, he'd hidden it well. I'd have to shut down the whole damn system until I had time to go through it properly.

I started bringing all of *Invictia's* defensive capabilities online. We were going to have to evade a ship designed for war. It was not going to be pretty.

A new connection came from the destroyer. I waited thirty seconds before answering it. I stared at my terminal and let my peripheral vision do the work. Commander Adams's enraged face once again filled the screen. "That was fast," I said. I made a point of looking up. "Oh, it's you again. Didn't we just have this conversation?"

"This is your final warning," he said.

"Okay, I'll play. Why should I surrender to you? The last time I was in your care, I wasn't exactly treated well." I pointed to my black eye. "So why would I choose to die slowly instead of quickly?"

"I give you my word that if you cooperate, you won't be harmed," he said with a smarmy smile.

"And Ari, my bodyguard?"

"Emperor Kos is a political prisoner. He will not be harmed as long as the Kos Empire accedes to the Quint Confederacy's demands for his release."

I rolled my eyes. "I'm sure Ari will be thrilled to learn she's become the Emperor of the Kos Empire."

In reality, Ari would be horrified. She wasn't actually my bodyguard—she was my head of security. She took her job seriously and she was going to be beyond pissed that I'd left her out of the loop.

"No more stalling," Adams said. "What is your decision?"

The stardrive still needed at least ten minutes to recharge, and even that was pushing it. Try to tunnel too early and the drive would overheat and fail catastrophically. But the odds that I could hold off a destroyer for ten minutes were also incredibly slim.

A ship of *Invictia's* size usually required a much longer recharge time, so Commander Adams might think he had time to attempt a capture before moving on to the big guns. Then again, he might just blow us to bits and be done with it.

Decisions, decisions.

"After careful consideration of all options," I said, "I'm going to have to decline your gracious invitation." My smile was all teeth. "If you want me, you'll have to catch me."

Commander Adams laughed. "You think you can avoid *Deroga*? You'll be dead after the first shot."

"Probably," I conceded. "But I'll take one of the Quint Confederacy's flagships down with me. Seems a decent way to go."

"And how exactly do you plan to take out a destroyer?" Adams asked.

"I'll guess you'll just have to wait and see," I said. "Enjoy hell."

I closed the connection before he could respond and enabled the ship's internal intercom. "I'm going to attempt to lose our Quint friends in the destroyer, but there's a tracker in *Invictia's* systems. I'm shutting down everything including life support, so prepare for zero gravity in five seconds."

Valentin let loose a string of curses so creative that I couldn't help but be impressed. "Don't get us killed," he said.

"I'll do my best," I said as I started shutting down the ship's systems. "It's going to get rough. We can tunnel in ten."

The harness kept me in the captain's chair as gravity died. I'd trained in zero gravity, as all pilots did, but it had been years since I'd used the training in practice. Life support systems were redundantly backed up so they didn't fail and no one turned them off for fun. I'd forgotten exactly how annoying zero gravity hair could be—mine drifted away from my head like Medusa's snakes.

I had to assume our entire route was compromised, so I changed the tunnel endpoint to the near side of CP57 and locked in the route. My system scan didn't show any activity, but that didn't mean anything. I changed the route again, moving it below CP57. This time I didn't lock it in, merely copied the coordinates. Then, I calculated a third point and locked it in.

I didn't know if any of these routes were being transmitted, or if it only transmitted when we tunneled, but I had to try to throw off our pursuers.

Warnings screamed across my screens as *Invictia* jerked hard to port. Apparently Commander Adams hadn't been joking about the whole killing us bit. I shut down route navigation and manually entered the coordinates I'd copied into the stardrive controls.

I disabled all of the remaining systems until we only had defense and piloting. I would drop those at the very last second.

Invictia was small and agile, but we were too close for it to make much difference. The autopilot flew us in a random pattern while the defensive systems did their very best to keep *Deroga's* weapons systems from locking on to us.

It was a losing proposition.

The ship shuddered and more warnings flashed as we took a direct hit the shields couldn't fully deflect. *Invictia* was a lightweight ship with minimal hull shielding. And if they breached our hull, we were done.

My world narrowed to watching for shots from the *Deroga* and twitching *Invictia* out of the path in the fraction of a second between seeing the pulse and it arriving. The autopilot reacted faster than I could, but it behaved in a predictable manner. I added an element of randomness that made predicting our moves more difficult.

Or so I told myself.

But with five minutes to go, it was clear we weren't going to make it. We'd taken a half-dozen hits and a third of the ship glowed red on my control screen.

"We're going to tunnel hot," I told Valentin over the open intercom. "If you believe in any deities, now would be a good time to ask for a miracle."

"How close are we?" he asked.

"Five minutes," I said and he groaned. Five minutes was right on the border between survivable and suicidal. "No choice," I said as *Invictia* shuddered again.

I overrode the stardrive's safety controls, then I timed the shots coming from *Deroga*. After we barely avoided the incoming pulse, I shut down every system on board except for the manual drive control. Another pulse lit up *Deroga* as I slammed my hand down on the tunneling override.

The ship lurched and the stars disappeared.

Then everything went dark.

7

I held my breath as *Invictia* diverted all available power into emergency cooling. The ship hummed with a subtle vibration as the stardrive's thermal control system radiated excess heat into space. The next thirty seconds would determine if we lived or died and there wasn't a damn thing I could do to tip the scales in our favor.

I unclipped my harness and pushed myself gently out of the chair. I kept a hand on the harness strap as I floated up. Zero gravity was fun for a minute, then it became a pain in the ass.

A gentle push sent me floating toward the door. While *Invictia* wasn't really designed for zero-g, it did have the bare minimum number of holds to make getting around possible. I hooked my toes under the foothold and used the manual override to push the door open.

I hissed out a breath as the movement pulled against my anchored leg. My *injured* anchored leg. Holy mother of gods, that *hurt*. The whimper escaped before I could suppress it.

"Samara, what's going on? Did we escape? Are you injured?" Valentin called from his cell.

"Tweaked my leg opening the door," I said. "I'm fine. And we haven't blown up yet, so maybe we'll survive after all."

The hallway had a waist-high handrail slot embedded into the wall. Usually it glowed like a soft nightlight when the overhead lights were off. Since all of the power was off, it appeared as a dark slash in the wall in the greenish gray of my night vision. I pushed toward the handrail and used it to pull myself down the hallway to the holding cells.

Valentin stood in the middle of his cell. If it wasn't for the floating bedding behind him, I'd think he had somehow retained gravity. As he walked closer to the thermoplastic wall separating us, I heard the faint clicking of the electromagnets in his mag-boots activating.

I hadn't realized that his boots *were* mag-boots. They were nearly as sleek as my leather boots. Proof, once again, that while money might not buy happiness, it could buy a lot of damn fine gear.

"Why are the lights out?" Valentin asked. "Are we stranded?"

"No," I said. I used the sides of the doorway to pull myself upright into a standing position. Without gravity, I hovered several centimeters above the floor. "The stardrive overheated and went into emergency shutdown. Once it cools off, everything should come back online." In theory.

"If you have a communication drone, I can have help here in twenty minutes," Valentin said.

Invictia did have a full quartet of communication drones. I wouldn't fly on a ship without them. Disabled ships in deep space could float around for decades before another ship happened upon them. Com drones had miniature stardrives so they could tunnel emergency messages back to populated space.

They were also incredibly expensive and single-use. I wasn't going to waste one just to bring the Kos Empire down on my head —especially not when we were already within communication range of CP57.

"I'll keep that in mind," I said. "For now, I'm going down to maintenance to see how bad it is."

"Samara, wait," Valentin said as I started to leave. He ran a frustrated hand through his hair before looking up and meeting my eyes. "Are your people truly starving?" he asked.

I pressed my lips together and struggled for patience. I wanted to rant, but that wouldn't get me anywhere. Valentin appeared to be willing to listen, so I needed to have a civilized conversation, even if diplomacy wasn't my strong suit.

"We were okay until your father's death last year," I said. "Then the war turned ugly, and both sides embargoed anyone who wasn't allied with them. Trade died overnight. Shipping and mercenary jobs, the lifeblood of our sector, also dried up. We can't grow enough food and we have no money to buy more. We've been on strict rations for the last six months."

Even with the rationing, we'd resorted to careful piracy just to stay alive, but we didn't have enough trained crews to bring in the amount of money and food we needed to feed everyone. And I didn't think Valentin would appreciate the reminder that I'd been stealing from him.

I sighed. "We have no income. The Coalition's coffers are empty, and Trigon Three isn't exactly a farmer's paradise. The last of our food supplies will run out within the next two months."

Growing food in the Trigon sector had always been more trouble than it was worth—it was far cheaper and easier to import food, right up until it wasn't. Lesson learned, but not quickly enough.

"Why not ally with one of the sides?" he asked. "I don't know about the Quint Confederacy, but we don't let our allies starve."

I wasn't entirely sure that was true, but I let it go. Instead, I said, "And be forced to join the war so many of my people risked their lives to escape? No."

In truth, I'd floated the idea three months ago. Every person I'd talked to had vehemently declared that they would rather starve, and after three months of rationing, they knew what they could expect.

Of course, they all assumed I would pull a miracle out of thin air, and I'd attempted to do just that. So far, my miracle was looking a little ragged around the edges.

"There must be something—" he started.

"There is. I'm doing it right now. Soon you'll be safe at home, and my people will get to eat for a while longer."

He stared at me for so long that I wasn't sure he was going to answer, but just as I was about to leave, he spoke. "I've spent the past eleven months dodging assassins and attempting to keep a fractured Empire functioning while trying to ferret out who is loyal to me and who is not. I was following up on a lead on one of my top-level advisors when I ran into Commander Adams."

I blinked at him in shock. If Valentin had been dodging paid hitmen, then the fact that he wasn't dead was a testament to both his luck and skill. Even excellent bodyguards were barely an obstacle to a determined assassin.

"I'm sorry I wasn't paying attention to how the war affected the neutral territories," he said. "I knew my advisors were feeding me false information, but it never occurred to me that they would lie about your sector."

"You knew your advisors were lying to you?"

He nodded, then the corner of his mouth tipped up in a grin. "I told you I wasn't incompetent or indifferent."

"You also said you didn't need my help," I reminded him drily. "Yet..." I waved at his cell.

"I'm working on it," he said. Before I could worry about that statement, his expression turned calculating. "My advisors won't pay for my return, but I'll pay you a million credits for your help if you let me go."

I laughed at him. "Even if your advisors won't pay, Quint will. They'll pay ten times that."

His eyes glinted in challenge as he stepped closer to the cell wall. "Three million if you help me figure out which advisors are loyal."

"That could take forever. I have my own sector to run. Nine million and your word that you won't declare war on us, and I'll drop you off in CP57—after the money clears, of course."

"Five million, I won't declare war on you, and it won't take more than three days."

"Eight million, half up front, no war, and I won't put my people in danger," I said. "How do you plan to figure out which advisors are loyal?"

He smiled and shook his head. "Seven million and you can find out."

Curiosity was a curse, but I didn't let it show on my face. "I'll think about it," I said. "But for now, I have to get the ship up and running."

"Please let me out," he said. "I've been cooped up for weeks."

"I'll think about it," I repeated. "Right now, I need to get *Invictia* back online in case Commander Adams shows up again."

————

AFTER A STOP by my quarters for my mag-boots, I headed down to maintenance. Slowly. Walking in mag-boots required a different set of muscle contractions than walking with gravity. With gravity, you pushed off the ground. Without gravity, the electromagnets in the soles of the mag-boots were the only thing holding you to the floor, so you had to pull yourself toward the ground with each step.

And having a busted-up thigh made it *excruciating,* even with the boots set to their lightest walking level.

I manually opened the door to the engine room and met a wall of heat. It was at least ten degrees warmer than the rest of the ship. My face burned like I had a fever. Well, this would be unpleasant.

By the time I made it to the main maintenance terminal, sweat clung to me in a thin sheet. If I moved too quickly, droplets drifted away like my own personal rain cloud. *Ugh.* I needed gravity, pronto.

I swiped my arms against my shirt to remove most of the sweat, then powered up the terminal and checked the diagnostics. The stardrive was still in the red zone. The system estimated it would be ten minutes before the drive dropped out of danger, then at least five hours before it would be recharged and cool enough to tunnel again.

The drive diagnostics showed some minor damage. It wasn't enough to prevent us from tunneling, but it would need to be repaired soon. Repair wouldn't be cheap; parts alone could run into tens of thousands of credits. It would have to wait until Kos paid me, one way or another.

Valentin's offer wasn't a bad one, assuming I could trust him. And that was still an open question. But for now, I had to deal with one problem at a time or I'd go crazy. Getting *Invictia* back online was my main concern.

I redirected some of the power from cooling back to the ship's most basic systems. The time to exit the red zone doubled, but the drive temperature didn't go up. The lights flickered on as *Invictia* sensed my presence in the room.

So far, so good.

With the lights on, the visual drive inspection would be far easier. I grabbed the checklist and lifted my heels, disengaging the electromagnets in my boots. I pushed off and floated up to the second-level walkway.

Using the walkway railing to spin around, I planted my feet on the ceiling. My boots engaged and I walked out over the stardrive enclosure. This might be the only use case where zero gravity was helpful because it was easier to see the top of the drive. Visual inspections very rarely turned up something the diagnostics had missed, but they were included on the checklist for a reason.

And you ignored the safety checklist at your own peril.

———

I COMPLETED the checklist and didn't find any additional issues. While I'd been busy, the stardrive had edged out of the red zone, though the room was still way too warm. My clothes were soaked through with sweat.

With the drive stabilizing, I could continue to reenable the ship's systems, but first I had to manually disable the communications array. I didn't know which system had Jax's tracker attached, but if I had to guess, it would be something vital like stealth or life support.

The system control box was plastered in dire warnings, all of which I ignored. This wasn't the first time I'd disabled this particular system. Inside, manual switches were neatly labeled with the functions they controlled.

I flipped the master communication array switch to the off position. In an abundance of caution, I also turned off the four secondary switches that controlled the individual antennas. I would have to turn them on again to send any outgoing messages, but I'd wait until just before our next tunnel transit.

I returned to the maintenance terminal and opened the intercom. "Life support will be returning in thirty seconds," I announced. "Prepare for gravity."

"Did you find the tracker?" Valentin asked.

"Not yet," I said.

"I'm good with software," Valentin said. "I could find it for you."

I rolled my eyes. Like I was letting him within three meters of my ship's systems. I'd be neck deep in Kos warships before I knew what happened. But the guy was persistent, I'd give him that.

I enabled the ship's stealth capability and then life support.

Gravity returned and I hissed out a curse as weight settled on my bad leg.

"What's wrong?" Valentin asked.

Shit, I'd left the intercom on. "Just my leg letting me know I'm still alive," I said. I changed the subject before he could respond. "We have about five hours until we can tunnel again. I'll let you know a few minutes before the transit. Until then, I'm shutting down the intercom."

"Wait—" he started.

I cut him off, then ran a quick system scan while I was still in the maintenance terminal. The ship's shielding was beat to hell, as were a few places in the hull where we'd come dangerously close to a breach. *Invictia* had kept us alive, but only just. She'd be in dry dock for weeks after this.

I powered off my mag-boots and headed back to the bridge. I needed to find the tracker. Plus, I had to decide whether I should trust the Emperor or continue with my original plan.

My only leverage was the Emperor himself. The Kos Empire had more than enough firepower to take out my fragile sector. I needed to ensure the path of least resistance was to pay me and move along, whatever form that took.

8

I glanced into Valentin's cell on my way past the door, then froze and backtracked. Another look confirmed what I had seen the first time—the cell was empty.

The hallway was clear. The door to medical was open, but the bridge and my quarters were both hidden behind closed doors. The bridge door should've been open.

I quietly moved to the door to my quarters. When it slid open, I peeked inside. The bedroom was empty but I couldn't see into the bathroom. I entered, keeping an eye on the door to the bathroom, but nothing moved.

I opened the wall panel that hid my armory. None of my weapons were missing. I pulled out an electroshock pistol and checked the magazine. I considered grabbing a plasma pistol as well, but if I couldn't take out Valentin with a magazine full of stun rounds, then things would be dire indeed.

I cleared the bathroom, then moved out into the hallway. I cleared the rec room again, followed by medical. Valentin was either on the bridge or hiding in the cargo bay, and I'd bet all of the imaginary credits we'd negotiated that he was on the bridge.

The door to the bridge slid open as I approached, surprising me enough that I stopped in my tracks.

Valentin looked up from the navigator's terminal and barely glanced at the pistol in my hand. Both of his hands were visible and he appeared unarmed.

"I found the tracker," he said calmly. "It was hidden deep in the life support code. You were right to turn everything off."

I brought the pistol up and he tensed but didn't move.

"How did you get out?" I asked quietly.

"I told you I'm good with software," he said with a grin that stopped just shy of cockiness.

I stepped into the room, keeping the electroshock pistol trained on him. "You were in an isolation cell."

"Not really," he said. "If you want true isolation, you need a Faraday cage. Software isolation can be defeated."

"Why didn't you lock the bridge door?"

"A locked door wouldn't have stopped you, but it *would've* pissed you off, making you more likely to shoot first. I'm not your enemy," he said. "I want to work with you."

"And you decided to prove that by escaping?"

"I could've escaped last night," he said, voice cool. "I could've locked you out of the bridge, taken control of your ship, and returned us directly to Koan while you slept." Koan was the Kos Empire's capital city on Achentsev Prime.

"So why didn't you?"

He ran a hand through his hair. "I considered it," he said honestly. "But once I calmed down, I realized you risked your life to rescue me from Commander Adams. You had your own motivation, but you still rescued me. Repaying that debt by stealing your ship would be dishonorable. And I have enough people who want me dead."

He seemed strangely sincere.

"What made you think I wouldn't just shoot you and be done with it?"

"Despite what I said yesterday, I've heard many things about you, Queen Rani, including that you are reasonable. Trust is a two-way street. If I didn't trust you to hear me out, I couldn't possibly ask you to trust me in return."

I tipped the pistol toward the floor. I could bring it up again in half a breath, but he was right that trust had to work both ways. "What is your plan and why is my help worth seven and a half million credits?"

He smiled but didn't contradict the amount. "Do we have a deal?" he asked.

"Will you pay four million up front?"

"If you insist," he said. At my nod, he continued, "Shall we shake on it?"

Trust was easier with a room between us and a pistol in my hand. Did I really trust him enough to let him close? I tried to think about what I'd heard about Valentin Kos. There wasn't much, but I'd never heard that he went back on his word, and that tended to get around faster than the opposite.

"I'd rather have a signed and sealed document," I said, "but I suppose a handshake is a start."

Valentin stood slowly. I transferred the pistol to my left hand. I could shoot with either hand, so it wasn't much of a sacrifice. I stood my ground and waited for him to come to me, so I could see if he had any concealed weapons.

His grin told me he knew exactly what I was doing, but he obligingly moved my way, being careful to stay nonthreatening. He stopped far enough away that I would have to take a step toward him, then he extended his hand. "If you help me with my advisor problem for a week maximum, I will pay you seven and a half million credits, four million up front, and I won't declare war on the Rogue Coalition without provocation."

"And whatever plan you're hatching won't put my people in danger," I reminded. He inclined his head in agreement.

Tension crawled up my spine, but trust had to start somewhere. And despite my claims, I had expected to get maybe five million for Emperor Kos. If he kept his word, seven and a half million was a good deal, especially with four up front.

I closed the remaining step between us and clasped his hand. His skin was warm and his grip was firm. This close, I could see the tension in his body. He was doing his utmost to look cool and calm, but he, too, found trust harder than his easy words made it appear.

After the universe's briefest handshake, I dropped his hand and stepped back. "Tell me your plan."

He smiled, and again I felt the pull of attraction. The man was dangerously handsome. He said, "It's your plan, actually. We're going to send my advisors the ransom request you planned to send."

When he didn't say anything else, I prompted, "And?"

"And we'll see how they respond. It might require a few follow-ups from you. We can wait here or in Arx, whichever you prefer."

"You agreed to pay me over seven million credits to send some *messages?*" I asked in disbelief. If so, it was the easiest job I'd ever taken.

"No," he said, and I braced myself for the real job. He continued, "The credits were for rescuing me from Commander Adams. The messages are just a bonus."

I blinked at him, feeling like I'd been played, but not exactly certain how.

"Before we work on the ransom message, do you want me to show you the location tracker?" he asked. "I haven't removed it yet because I didn't want to change your ship's code without your permission."

I nodded and followed him back to the navigator's terminal. I knew just enough about software to get myself in trouble, but if Valentin could disable the tracker for now, I could have an expert go through the code in Arx to ensure Valentin didn't leave me any surprises.

He pulled up the system code for the carbon dioxide scrubber and scrolled down through the file. "Whoever did this was clever and covered their tracks well," he said with a note of admiration. He highlighted two lines. "This is the change." He then launched into a detailed explanation that I only barely followed. "Do you want me to fix it?" he finally asked.

"Yes," I said. "We'll need to be able to use the communication array without bringing Commander Adams down on our head. He already knows where I'm heading, so we will have to wait for your responses in Arx. I want to be there if he attacks."

Luckily for me, even a destroyer couldn't tunnel straight to Trigon Three from our last location. If Commander Adams did decide to follow us to Arx, by the time he arrived, he'd find a few nasty surprises waiting for him. The Rogue Coalition might not be able to hold off an army, but a single destroyer was well within our capability.

"Arx is fine," Valentin said as his hands flew over the terminal.

"You know that if you betray me, I'll kill you, right?" I asked. "And I'll be far more successful than the assassins who have tried so far."

He paused and met my eyes. "I know," he said simply.

I nodded at him. Now that the adrenaline was wearing off, my thigh throbbed with pain. I needed another dose of painkiller, but no way was I taking it with Valentin running around loose. I'd have to deal.

I moved to the captain's chair and lowered myself into the seat with a silent hiss.

But not silent enough, apparently. "Are you in pain?" Valentin asked.

"I have a gaping hole in my thigh," I said drily. "What do you think?"

He glanced at me and understanding dawned across his face. "And you're not going to take more painkillers, are you?"

"Not until we're in Arx," I confirmed. It would be a miserable few hours, but I'd survived worse. I needed all of my wits because I only trusted him so far.

"I need a few more minutes here. Why don't you start on the ransom message? Write whatever you were planning to send before."

I started on the message but kept an eye on him. Eventually, he finished with the tracker and started helping, but he remained in the navigator's chair. I appreciated the distance.

It took an hour and a half of constant revision before Valentin and I were both happy with the wording. I demanded a ten million credit payment for the safe return of Emperor Kos. I worked in a few subtle threats, but mostly I spun it as a finder's fee.

While we waited for the stardrive to cool down and recharge, I wrote a second message to my advisors to let them know what was going on. I'd likely arrive before most of them read it, but if anything went wrong with the next transit they'd at least know I didn't vanish into the ether on purpose.

With nothing to do but wait and dwell on the throbbing in my thigh, I turned to Valentin for a distraction. "Why do you keep advisors you know are disloyal?"

"It's not as easy as that," he said. "They have been playing the game for a very long time. They are careful and crafty. And I can't afford to be wrong."

"I figured for seven point five million credits you were going to ask me to quietly take a few of them out," I said.

"Would you have?"

"Maybe," I said honestly. "I thought that part of my life was behind me, but that many credits would have fed my people for years."

Some people would argue I had no soul, that I'd forfeited it the first day I accepted a kill contract. But while my soul might be warped or missing, I still had a personal code of honor and a set of morals that, while not entirely lawful, were mine nonetheless.

It had been a very long time since I'd killed someone under contract that I later regretted. That stain would never wash away, but it had forced me to do my research meticulously and to ensure each target would get exactly what I thought they deserved. If I had doubts, I walked away. Just because Valentin thought his advisors needed to be killed wouldn't be a good enough reason on its own.

"Why didn't you shoot me when you found me on your bridge?" he asked.

"Surprise, mostly," I said. "I was trying to figure out how stupid you were for forgetting to lock the door. Then you were just sitting there." I shrugged. "If you had so much as twitched, I would've shot you. But you didn't."

The conversation drifted into silence, and I let it go. I let myself slip into a half doze. *Invictia* would alert me if anything needed my attention, and I had long ago learned to wake from this state at the softest sound, so I didn't need to worry about Valentin sneaking up on me.

The time passed quietly. My mind wandered to Valentin. He wasn't at all what I had expected. He was far smarter and more cunning than I had believed—far more handsome, too.

Instead of putting me off, the little glimpses of craftiness only made him more interesting because I found the lion far more compelling than the lamb. I might admire a handsome man, but if he didn't have a brain to back up his beauty, the attraction quickly faded.

That was not going to be a problem with Valentin, for better or worse.

Invictia chimed to let me know that the stardrive was ready. I reluctantly pulled my thoughts back to the task at hand, then stood and stretched. My thigh ached with a deep, stabbing pain, and I still had to go all the way back down to the maintenance area to turn on the communication array again.

Valentin had been leaned back in the navigator's chair, but he sat up and blinked sleepily at me when I started moving.

"I'm going down to maintenance to turn on the antennas," I said. My first step hurt, but I absolutely refused to let anything show on my face.

He snapped up straight. "Let me do it," he said, standing. "You don't want to leave me alone on the bridge, do you?"

I raised an eyebrow at him. I knew exactly what he was doing, but I was going to let him get away with it because it felt like a hot poker was lodged in my right thigh. "Okay," I agreed. "I'll turn on the intercom, so I can walk you through it."

9

After Valentin turned on the communication array, we sent the ransom message to the advisors he specified. I also sent the message I'd written to my advisors.

Because we were within communication range of CP57, Valentin was able to instantly transfer the first half of my payment into my account. I stared at the number in disbelief, still halfway sure that it would disappear like smoke if I looked away.

"I can't believe you actually followed through," I said at last.

"I keep my promises," he said.

"Then we have that in common," I said. My respect for him rose a notch. "Strap in. We're going to tunnel close to Trigon Three, so we'll be landing soon."

He pulled the navigator's harness over his shoulders and I did the same in the captain's chair. I pulled up the navigation control and entered our tunnel endpoint.

The transit was smooth and uneventful. We came out the other side under full power. *Invictia* had been bruised but not broken. I loved this little ship.

Less than a minute after the transit, an inbound communication request came through on the Rogue Coalition's encrypted channel. I accepted on my terminal and Ari's irate face appeared on screen.

A statuesque blond in her early thirties, Ari was stunning even in anger. I joked that I wanted to be just like her when I grew up, even though she was only two years older than me. She always told me I had about twenty centimeters to go.

"Where have you been for the last week?" she demanded. "And why aren't you answering neural links? Have you turned traitor?" My head of security was not one to mince words. She was also one of my closest friends.

"Hello, Ari," I drawled just to watch her scowl deepen. "Did you get my message?"

She frowned. "No."

The Rogue Coalition's com system was not exactly top-of-the-line. It didn't surprise me that I'd arrived before the message. It was another reason I'd decided to stop at a communication hub to send the ransom request.

"I've rescued the Kos Emperor and we're working together for the next week. The Quint mercs I stole him from did not appreciate my interference, so it's liable to get a little hot here. Make sure everyone knows the evacuation plan and what to do in case of attack."

We had too many people in Arx and not enough places for them to go for a full-scale evacuation, but maybe a few could get clear. "Anyone who can shelter with friends or family at another settlement for a few days should leave now."

Ari didn't even blink, she just started typing commands on her terminal. "Anything else?" she asked.

"I have reason to believe an unflagged Quint destroyer called the *Deroga* might make an appearance soon. We need to make it feel unwelcome. Also, some Kos ships may show up. Don't attack unless they start it." I wasn't sure if Valentin had sent any other messages, but I felt it best to cover all of our bases.

"Anything else?" she asked again, eyebrows raised.

"I'm not a traitor."

That brought back the scowl. "Anything *else*, like how you got that shiner? Or maybe an apology for leaving your head of security behind while you went off to do something incredibly stupid and dangerous?"

"Stupid, dangerous, and *successful*. That last one makes all the difference," I said. She would eventually get the story from me, but for now I wasn't going to volunteer just how close it had been. "I needed someone to keep an eye on things while I was gone."

"You have half a dozen advisors who would jump at the chance."

"Yes, but I trust you the most."

She rolled her eyes. "Hurry up and get on the ground so I can kick your ass." She paused as she seemed to remember the rest of what I'd said. "You're working with Emperor Kos? How is the advisory council going to feel about that?"

"I have seven point five million reasons why they'll be thrilled," I said, "but keep that number to yourself for now."

Her eyes widened. It took a lot to surprise Ari but I'd just managed it. I hid my grin.

"Call an advisory council meeting for tomorrow. We'll make a list of priority purchases." I paused. "Actually, don't mention that. Just call the meeting."

Ari inclined her head. "I'll get your orders sent out and then meet you at your hangar. Don't leave the ship until I'm there."

"Yes, ma'am," I said with a mock salute. "See you soon."

She nodded and cut the link.

With all of the ship's systems back online, *Invictia* didn't need my input to land. I stayed in the captain's seat anyway because there was always the possibility of an anomaly.

From a distance, Trigon Three was a gray rock half covered in gray oceans. Up close, it wasn't much better. Centuries ago, it had been terraformed just enough that humans could survive on its barren surface, but a lush utopia it was not. Most of the settlements were underground to escape the howling wind and bitter cold.

Invictia dropped roughly through the atmosphere, aiming for the spaceport at Arx, the Rogue Coalition's headquarters and the main city on Trigon Three. There were a few other settlements on the planet, but their locations were more closely guarded.

The Rogue Coalition had slowly been absorbing planets in this sector but Trigon Three was our public face. I did my best to draw all eyes here so our other settlements were safer.

At a particularly vicious bump, Valentin grunted. "You weren't kidding about strapping in. Is it always this rough?"

"No, it seems the compensators were damaged in our little firefight. Hang tight, we'll be down in a few."

As if to contradict me, the ship lurched sideways. My harness dug into my shoulders and my thigh banged against the side of my chair. I cursed the air blue. It was either that or pass out. When I paused for breath, I found Valentin grinning at me. "Very creative," he said with approval.

The spaceport was a cluster of low, gray buildings on the vid screens. A few ships were parked on landing pads, but most were in the underground hangar.

Arx itself used to be a military base, so it was built for utility rather than beauty. The few surface buildings were low-slung plascrete monoliths with minimal windows. The underground levels weren't much better, all straight lines and white walls. One of the first things I'd done as queen was install daylight simulators and ceiling panels that mimicked clear blue skies in the common areas.

One privilege of queendom was a private underground hangar that was connected via underground hallway to the main base areas and my residence. As *Invictia* approached, the hangar doors slid open. We slowly dropped down to the landing pad below.

Invictia settled on the ground and the engines cut out. The vid screens showed Ari waiting at the entrance with a quartet of soldiers. I lowered the cargo ramp and she headed our way. I unbuckled my harness and stood gingerly. My leg throbbed like a bitch.

"Stay quiet and don't do anything stupid," I told Valentin. "Ari doesn't play around with strangers."

He nodded. I turned toward the door and waited for the inquisition to hit.

———

"SAMARA!" Ari called.

"On the bridge," I called back. I still hadn't enabled my neural links, mostly because I still wasn't sure using them with Valentin around was a good idea, but not being able to link was a pain.

"Where is the Emperor?" Ari asked as she entered the room. She had on her work clothes—black utility pants and a tank top. Today's tank was bright blue.

Despite the fact that even the underground rooms in Arx tended toward chilly, Ari rarely wore long sleeves. She was from a frozen planet that made Trigon Three look like a tropical paradise. After three years, her internal thermometer still hadn't adjusted.

Valentin's eyes widened at the sight of her. She had that effect on people. Tall, slender, and gorgeous, you'd never know from looking that a hard-ass lurked under her pretty blonde exterior.

Said hard-ass looked me over. "You're lucky that you're injured," she said at last, "or I really would kick your ass."

"I appreciate your restraint," I deadpanned. I half-turned to Valentin. "Ari, meet Emperor Valentin Kos. Valentin, meet Arietta Mueller, my head of security."

"It's a pleasure, Ms. Mueller," Valentin said with a charming grin and a short bow.

Ari scowled at him. "Save it. If you must address me, call me

Ari. Keep your hands where I can see them and don't wander off without an escort. We clear?"

This time, Valentin's smile was genuine. "We're clear," he said.

I decided to take Valentin along while I checked in with my people. My trust in him was far more solid when he was in sight. And taking him along would give him a first-hand view of the consequences of his empire's stupid war.

"Anything in particular need my attention?" I asked Ari.

"Nothing urgent," she said.

"Then I'm heading to the market," I said. "I've been gone too long. I need to see everyone. I'll take Valentin with me." I didn't expect anarchy, but I always made it a point to stop by the market after an absence. It gave people a chance to see me and let me know about any concerns that had arisen while I was gone.

Ari tensed as Valentin stepped close to my side. He touched my arm. When I turned to him, his gray eyes were solemn and his warm scent wrapped around me. I stood rooted and wary as he ghosted his fingers over my bruised cheek. It would be so, so easy to fall under his spell. "You need to visit medical."

"I will when I have time," I said. My voice came out huskier than I would've liked. I cleared my throat and forged on. "I'll be okay for now."

Ari raised her eyebrows at me. She didn't say anything, but I did not like the speculative gleam in her eye.

"First, we're going to need to disguise Valentin," I said with a glance at him. He'd washed the dried blood off his face, but the bruises remained. The stubble shadowing his jaw helped, but he still looked too much like himself. "I'd rather not have to fight off a mob to keep him safe."

"You give yourself too little credit," Ari said. "The people may hate the Emperor, but they respect you. They wouldn't mob you."

"I'd rather not put it to the test," I said. "We'll head to my place first, followed by the market.

I led, Valentin followed, and Ari brought up the rear. The four soldiers she'd brought waited for us on the cargo ramp. Lieutenant Peters saluted as I approached. I'd told him time and again that it wasn't necessary, but he just smiled, nodded, and carried on doing exactly as he pleased. The three soldiers behind him copied his behavior.

"Welcome home, your majesty," he said gravely. He usually only busted out the title for formal occasions. Either Ari had briefed him or he recognized Emperor Kos.

"I see you're in fine form today, Lieutenant," I said with the wave that was as close as I got to a salute. His formal facade cracked, and he grinned at me. I clutched dramatically at my chest. "Watch where you aim that thing, soldier. You'll give a lady ideas."

Malcolm Peters was fifty if he was a day, but he could still stop traffic with a smile. Add in beautiful ebony skin, a few interesting scars, and distinguished, close-cropped gray hair, and women, young and old, fell over themselves to knock on his door to see if he needed anything—*anything at all.*

It was a source of great amusement for the rest of us, and Malcolm put up with our gentle ribbing with aplomb, pretending ignorance while he played along.

Unfortunately, today my traditional opening line bordered on a lie. Soldiers were given larger rations to make up for their extra physical effort, but even so, Malcolm had lost weight.

I couldn't even keep the men and women who'd volunteered to put themselves between us and danger fit and healthy. *Never again,* I silently vowed.

10

W hen I became Queen, I took over the former base
commander's house. It had one floor above ground
as well as two below ground. The lowest under-
ground floor was on the same level as the rest of the base, so it
became a public space. People who needed to talk to me or just
wanted to hang out could come and go as they pleased.

I'd had my bedroom above ground until the rationing started
and I could no longer justify heating the whole floor just so I
could have a window. When I'd moved my personal rooms to the
middle floor, most of the stuff that had been stored there had
moved to other storage locations. But because someone always
needed something, I had a supply closet of spare clothes.

We took the private stairs up to my rooms, bypassing the
public area entirely. I stopped on the landing for the middle floor
with Ari, Valentin, and Malcolm. Ari had dismissed the three
extra soldiers, but she'd asked Malcolm to stay for Valentin's
"security detail."

She wasn't fooling any of us, but we all played along.

While I didn't mind if Valentin saw the public parts of Arx, I'd
prefer it if he didn't have a detailed mental map of my personal

space, temporary truce or not. I turned to him. His expression was distant, indicating he was focusing on a neural link. "Wait here," I said. He barely acknowledged me.

I glanced at Ari. She nodded and leaned against the stairwell wall. Standing straight, she was as tall as Valentin, and they would make a striking couple. Luckily for me, Ari's wife would have something to say about that, and Stella Mueller was not a woman to cross lightly.

I let myself into my rooms the old-fashioned way, with a handprint and face scan. Usually I'd connect through the net, but I was still offline. I wasn't sure if a net connection was safe from Valentin, but I would have to connect sooner rather than later because I expected a reply from the Kos Empire. Once they replied, I could get Valentin to hand over the rest of the credits he owed me and then send him on his way.

Digging through the supply closet, I found a few items that looked big enough to fit Valentin. It wasn't unusual for newcomers to wear a coat, hat, and scarf until they got used to the chill, so he wouldn't stand out.

While I had access to my closet, I took the time to put on a base layer under my shirt. The cold didn't usually bother me, but thanks to the blood loss, I'd felt it more on the walk from the ship. I needed to rehydrate as soon as possible, but until then, there was no reason to be miserable.

I gathered up the extra clothes and returned to the stairwell. No one had moved. A faint frown marred Valentin's brow, but his still unfocused expression meant that it was likely from a neural link or net connection.

"Put these on," I said. I held out the clothes I'd found.

He flashed me a grin and reached to take the clothes and put them on. With the old coat on, hat pulled low, and scarf wrapped around his neck, he was less Emperor Kos and more homeless refugee. Good enough.

We started down the stairs. Ari caught me up on the public

news that I'd missed while I'd been gone. The private news would have to wait until we didn't have Valentin in the audience.

Ari said we were burning through our food even faster than expected. The advisory council had approved stricter rationing, effective immediately. We had crews out looking for supplies, but none of them had solid targets yet.

"How did people take the news?" I asked.

Ari shrugged. "Nobody was thrilled, but there wasn't too much outcry. They know you're doing everything in your power. Everyone is pitching in where they can."

The Rogue Coalition had its problems, just like any large group of people, but when the going got tough, the tough got deadly determined. After I had made it abundantly, *painfully* clear that I wouldn't tolerate people taking advantage of one another, they decided that their energy was better spent trying to figure out how to stick it to Kos and Quint.

But that goodwill would only take us so far. If starvation ever truly set in, the Coalition would collapse into a horde of wolves that only looked out for number one. At that point, there would be nothing I could do except try to direct the fury away from the most vulnerable.

"Okay, let's go see what I can do to help," I said.

———

OCCUPYING the former military base's central parade grounds, the market was the largest communal gathering place in Arx. The panels overhead made it appear like we were under bright blue skies with slowly drifting white clouds, but only the front half were on.

A few solid buildings had sprung up in the open space—the bakery and general store, for example—but mostly small market stalls leaned against one another, built with whatever was handy.

In the distance, under the dark half of the ceiling, shadows clung to the walls and narrow pathways.

It reminded me of the back-alley markets on the planet I'd grown up on.

Many of the stalls were empty now, but the market still buzzed with activity. People might not have much money, but that didn't prevent them from getting together to gossip and barter.

Zita O'Neill caught sight of us first. "Samara, you're back!" She pulled me into a hug and kissed the air next to my cheek. Then she stepped back and glanced behind me. Her smile turned coy. "And you brought Lieutenant Peters, how lovely."

A matronly woman in her forties with red ringlets and a ready smile, Zita ran Arx's main bakery. She'd been a fixture in Arx from the beginning, but these days she made simple bread for rations and none of the fancy little desserts she loved.

I'd been in and out of Arx for the past month tracking down Valentin, so I hadn't seen Zita for weeks. She, too, had lost more weight. The last of the cherubic roundness had disappeared from her cheeks, and it made her look worn and tired, like she'd aged five years in five weeks.

"Hello, Zita," I said. "I missed you. Did you keep everyone out of trouble while I was gone?"

She laughed. "You're the only one who has the power to work that particular miracle, but I did my best." She paused, then looked surprised. "You're not accepting neural links?" she asked quietly.

"Not right now," I said.

She nodded, then leaned in and whispered, "I snuck the Dovers' girl some extra bread. She's pregnant but won't tell her pa, so she can't get the extra rations."

I appreciated her discretion, but Ari could hear a person breathing two rooms away thanks to her augments, and she wasn't the only one with augmented senses. Secrets rarely stayed secret in Arx.

"That's fine," I said. "I'll check on her." I'd watched Lily Dovers grow up. She was barely eighteen. As far as I knew, she had a good relationship with her father, so she should have no reason to hide her pregnancy.

If Lily had been forced, I'd make her assailant a very public, very gruesome example of why trying that shit in my sector was mortally stupid. The seedier elements of the Coalition tended to self-police, and I let a lot of things slide, but I had a zero tolerance policy on rape, murder, and domestic abuse across the board.

"Do you have time for tea?" Zita asked.

"I wish I did, but I have to show Val here around," I said.

Zita barely spared him a glance. Outsiders weren't shunned, largely because everyone here had been an outsider at one point or another, but they weren't welcomed with open arms either. "Come back when you have time," she said to me.

"I will," I promised.

"Val?" Valentin asked softly when we were far enough away.

"I didn't disguise you just to shout your full name to everyone nearby."

Then there was no more time to talk because we were to the next group of people. As they crowded around us, I latched onto Valentin's right arm so we wouldn't be separated.

Arx had nearly eight thousand permanent residents and another two thousand newcomers who were waiting to transition to another settlement. I tried my best to meet every group who came to the city. This gave them the chance to ask questions and gave me the chance to lay down the rules and see their faces.

Thanks to some quirk in my brain, I had excellent facial memory, so I recognized everyone around us, even if I couldn't remember their names. All of their faces were leaner than the last time I'd seen them.

As we moved through the market, most of the questions were about the new ration levels: did I know about them, how long would we be at this level, what was I doing to fix it. I answered them patiently: yes, not long, I have a plan.

A young mother clutching an infant hovered on the edge of the crowd. She was fairly new to Arx, and she'd lost a dramatic amount of weight in the short time she'd been here. "Excuse me," I said to the people around me. Her eyes widened as Valentin and I moved toward her but she stood her ground. Smart woman.

"Walk with me," I said to her. "What's your name again?"

Valentin was a silent shadow at my side.

"It's Patricia, um, your highness," she stammered.

I laughed. "Samara is fine," I said. "We don't stand on ceremony around here too much. What about your baby?"

"His name is Joseph," she said with obvious pride.

"It's a good name," I said. When we'd put a little distance between us and the crowd, I stopped and turned to her. "Why aren't you eating your rations?"

She looked me straight in the eyes and lied. "I am," she said.

I raised an eyebrow and waited.

She looked away and blushed. "My little girl is always hungry. Sometimes I share my rations with her."

"You've lost too much weight. If you keep this up, you won't be able to nurse Joseph, and where will that leave him? You're to get double rations for two weeks, tell Zita and Eddie and they'll confirm it with me. Eat every bite of your own rations—no sharing. I expect to see a marked improvement in your weight the next time we talk."

She ducked her head. "Yes, my lady," she said.

"If your daughter is hungry all the time, get her checked in medical. If nothing is wrong, come and see me and we'll see if we need to adjust the children's rations."

Children's rations were a dear subject to me. When I'd first joined the Rogue Coalition, I'd been perfectly happy looking out for number one and ignoring everything around me—until I'd noticed a little boy starving to death while everyone turned a blind eye. My rusty conscience had groaned to life and set me on the path to becoming Queen.

Patricia looked up with hope in her eyes. "You would adjust the rations?" she asked. At my nod, she bowed deeply and I wondered at her background. "Thank you, Queen Samara. I will not forget this." She hurried off, as if afraid that I'd change my mind if she lingered.

"Want me to let Zita and Eddie know?" Ari asked.

"Please," I said. "And I want someone to check on Patricia in three days. Make sure it really is her little girl that's getting her rations."

"I'll have Imogen handle it. She's good with people," Ari said.

"Have her talk to Lily Dovers, too," I said. I would've liked to talk to Lily myself, but I had to deal with Valentin first. "If Lily refuses to talk to her or if Imogen suspects anything, let me know and I'll deal with it."

"Do you always take this much interest in your citizens' lives?" Valentin asked. His expression had been attentive as we'd made our way through the market.

"She does," Ari grumbled. "Do you know how many times I've heard complaints about rations? They're adults; they shouldn't whine like children."

"Arietta, be nice," I warned. I'd heard this argument before. But if bitching to me about rations made people feel better, then I would endure it to keep the peace. With any luck, this would be the last time I had to hear about it for a while.

"She's right, you know. They're adults. You shouldn't let them walk all over you. They'll lose respect for you," Valentin said.

"I've been Queen for five years and in five years, I've had exactly zero coup attempts. You've been Emperor for what, eleven months? How many attempted coups have *you* had?"

Valentin refused to answer, which was answer enough.

"It seems to me," I said, "that if anyone here should be giving another person leadership advice, it should be *me* teaching *you*. I'm available any time at quite an exorbitant rate, but I'll give you a ten percent discount due to your dire need."

11

It took another twenty minutes to extract myself from the market after my chat with Patricia. My thigh throbbed like fire had replaced my bones, slowly burning me from the inside out.

When a little boy ran up to give me a farewell hug, I wasn't fast enough to dodge. He clamped his little arms around my bad thigh and gave me a squeeze. Tears sprang to my eyes and I clenched my jaw hard enough that my teeth ached.

He beamed up at me, and I somehow summoned a smile. I ruffled his hair, then he darted away with a wave, unaware of just how much pain he had caused. After he disappeared from view, I hissed out a breath.

"Are you okay?" Valentin asked. I realized that my hand had gone white-knuckled around his arm and I consciously loosened my grip.

"Give me a second," I wheezed.

"You need to visit medical," Ari said.

"I will as soon as I have time," I promised again. An auto-doc could patch me up in a few hours, but I had to have a few hours where I could afford to stay put in medical.

Ari leveled her hard stare at me. "See that you do, or I'll rat you out to Stella."

My horrified expression was only half-feigned. "Let's not be hasty now," I said with a placating wave. Ari's wife ran medical. Most of the time, Stella Mueller was the nicest lady you'd ever meet. But she ran medical like she had a doctorate in dictatorship. She wasn't afraid to restrain unruly patients—Queens included. If Stella caught wind of how badly I was injured, she'd hunt me down.

Ari's smile had a slightly evil edge to it and Malcolm laughed. I glared at both of them, but I had to suppress the smile that threatened to break through. "With friends like you, I hardly need enemies," I sniffed.

"We prefer you alive, your majesty," Malcolm said, "because stars know we don't want your job." He shuddered in mock horror and Ari nodded in agreement. It *was* easier to not have any coup attempts when no one wanted the job in the first place.

Before I could change the subject to something safer, Valentin's stomach growled. It was a little early for dinner, but someone would be in the mess hall anyway.

"Come on," I said. "I need to eat, too." It would give me a chance to sit and rest my leg.

"Hey, Eddie, how's it going?" I asked as we stepped up to the counter in the mess hall.

Eddie Tarlowski looked up with a grin. He was twenty-five, with shaggy blond hair and a forgettable face. He had been one of the best thieves in the universe until he'd gotten caught by the Quint Confederacy and conscripted. He'd escaped, but not before he lost an arm and a leg in some nameless skirmish with the Kos Empire in deep space.

Two years ago, he'd shown up in Arx with two mechanical

limbs and a chip on his shoulder the size of Andromeda. He'd spent most of his first six months peeling potatoes as punishment for everything from stealing to trying to incite a riot.

I'd begun to wonder if he was ever going to let go of his anger.

Then, slowly, so slowly, he'd warmed up to the chef and starting appearing in the kitchen without it being a punishment. Now, he was the head chef—though, much like Zita, he hadn't been able to flex his surprisingly good culinary muscles in months.

"Long time, no see, boss," he said. "You bring me any of that steak I asked for?"

"I'm afraid not," I said with true regret. I hadn't had real meat in nearly a year. "What's on the dinner menu?"

"You're in for a treat tonight," Eddie said. "I've made my famous *risotto di proteine*."

I laughed. "At least it sounds delicious. I need two servings, one for me and one for Val here," I said, jerking a thumb at Valentin. "He's not in the system yet, so you can deduct his from my rations."

"Sure thing, boss," Eddie said. He pulled out two bowls with his gray mechanical arm. These days, Eddie used the arm so naturally that, if you couldn't see the color, you wouldn't know it was mechanical. But we'd lost a lot of dishes before he'd calibrated the strength correctly.

Eddie added two ladlefuls of protein mush to each bowl. It had all of the nutrients required to keep you alive, which was the nicest thing you could say about it. He pulled out a tray and set the bowls on it, then sliced an apple in half and put a half next to each bowl. "Bon appétit," he said with a flourish.

"Thanks, Eddie," I said.

I reached for the tray, but Valentin beat me to it. When I didn't move, he tilted his head toward the tables.

I stopped to add two glasses of water to the tray, then led Valentin to a table in sight of the door. I'd left Ari and Malcolm outside so they didn't have to watch us eat up close. Despite their protests that it was fine, I knew how hard it was to do so when you were hungry.

The mess hall was nearly empty. In another hour it would be packed, but for now we had the place to ourselves. I sat down with a grateful groan.

Valentin put the tray on the table and sat across from me. "You really should go to medical," he said quietly.

"After I send you home, I will," I said. I met his eyes. "Who have you been communicating with?" I asked frankly.

Valentin smiled and my heart kicked.

"Your com system is terrible," he said. "I can't seem to link through it, and I've sent messages, but I haven't received any responses. Are you sure you'll know when my advisors contact you?"

"Yes," I said. "It may take an extra hour or two, but the system isn't *that* bad."

I pulled my bowl toward me. Protein mush had a texture somewhere between oatmeal, risotto, and engine grease. The taste was not much better. Valentin eyed his bowl as if he expected it to attack.

"Eat up," I said. "It's not delicious, but it's not poisonous, either."

"I'm familiar with PRiMeR," he said, using the official acronym for Protein Rich Meal Replacement. "I just hoped to never see it again."

That surprised me. PRiMeR was far, far down the list of possible meal replacements. It was one of the cheapest you could buy. Someone as rich as the Emperor should never have had a reason to dip below the specialty MREs produced for the elite classes.

It was on the tip of my tongue to ask him about it, to peel back the layers to find the real Valentin Kos, but I swallowed the question. I already liked him too much, but despite his friendly attitude, we were not friends. At best, we were temporary allies.

We finished our meal in silence. With nothing better to do, I decided to check on the guest suite near my quarters. It was originally intended for visiting dignitaries, but we hadn't had any of those in the entire time I'd lived in Arx.

I think we'd converted the suite into storage, but if we were lucky, it would work for a night or two while Valentin was here. I wasn't letting him hang out in my rooms, and I didn't quite trust him enough to leave him on his own, so a shared suite would have to do.

Now I just had to convince him it wasn't a cell in disguise.

———

ONCE I TOLD Ari that I planned to clean out the guest suite, she rounded up a few people to help. To my surprise, even Valentin pitched in. I carried boxes and moved furniture until my leg screamed with pain and threatened to collapse.

Ari caught me grimacing and leaning against the wall. "If your butt isn't in a chair in the next two minutes," she said, "I'm calling Stella."

"I'm okay," I tried.

She gave me her hard stare and crossed her arms. I started to say something else, but she held up her hand. "I'll watch your man," she said. "Butt in chair, now."

I wasn't going to touch the "your man" comment, so I retreated to the living room and sank into one of the chairs we'd uncovered with a grateful sigh. My thigh felt like living fire. I silently admitted that I might have pushed myself too far.

While resting, I enabled my neural links and connected to the net. The familiar hum of information in the back of my mind felt like reconnecting with a long-lost friend.

I scanned the news, but there was no mention of the Kos

Emperor's escape. Commander Adams either hadn't told his superiors or they were keeping it quiet. We needed to get Valentin home and into the news before Quint had time to launch an attack on Arx. One destroyer we could handle, but a full-on assault would flatten us.

With that in mind, I checked my messages. And there, right on top, was a response from the Kos Empire. I read it twice, then sent a copy to the terminal in my office for safekeeping.

The Kos Empire had just offered me ten million credits to kill Valentin Kos.

I opened a neural link to Ari. *Is at least one bedroom habitable?*

Yes, she replied. *We're working on the second one now.*

Don't bother, I can sleep on the sofa. Please clear the suite and ask Valentin to join me in the living room. You might as well call Stella, too. I'll need advice from both of you.

I'm on it, she said and closed the link.

I waved and thanked the people who had helped us as they passed through the living room on their way to the door. Ari and Valentin were the last to appear.

"Did you get a response?" Valentin asked.

"Yes, link me your address and I'll send you a copy. We're waiting on one more person before we discuss it."

Ari flopped down on the sofa across from me. "Stella is on her way," she said. "She was in medical, so it'll be a few minutes."

Valentin sent me his address. He wasn't using his official Kos Empire account. I sent him a copy of the message and also forwarded it to Stella and Ari. I glanced at him. "Is one of the bedrooms clean enough that you won't mind using it for a few days?"

He frowned, his eyes distant as he read the response. "Either bedroom is fine," he said absently. "They are both far nicer than where I've been for the last few weeks." His expression flickered to something dark and angry before he smoothed it out into a polite mask. "In fact, if it's going to be a few minutes, do you mind if I take a shower? I found some spare clothes that should work."

It was clear that he wanted some time alone to deal with the impact of his advisors' treachery. It was one thing to *think* you were being betrayed; it was another thing altogether to have it confirmed.

"Of course you can shower. I'm sorry. I should've asked you earlier."

I scanned his body. I remembered the muscles in his back—how would the rest of him look? I belatedly realized what I was doing and yanked my gaze back up to his face. He grinned at me, his expression warm.

"Don't worry about it," he said. I wasn't sure if he was talking about my apology or my wandering eyes, but I chose not to ask for clarification. He turned toward the bedroom and tossed over his shoulder, "I'll be quick."

As soon as the bedroom door clicked shut, Ari raised an eyebrow. I gave her my most innocent smile. "What?" I asked.

"You looked like you would happily scrub his back if only he would ask. What's going on?"

"I have eyes, and he's gorgeous. He's also smart and clever. If he were anyone else, I would be trying to get just such an invite." I sighed. "I like him. I didn't expect to and it's messing with my brain."

"How sure are you that he isn't just stalling until his troops get here?"

"How close is Stella?" I asked.

"I'll link her in."

I nodded and briefly explained my original plan to ransom Valentin, how he'd escaped from his cell, and our agreement.

"You think he's trustworthy?" Ari asked.

I thought about it for a moment. "I think he will keep his word," I said slowly, "but I think he's far smarter than he tries to appear."

12

Stella let herself in after a brief knock. She joined us in the living room. She was several centimeters taller than me, with rich brown skin, dark eyes, and long dark hair. People mistook us for sisters, which I took as an extreme compliment because Stella was beautiful. She and Ari made a strikingly gorgeous couple.

I waved to her but didn't get up. Stella took one look at me and pulled a med scanner seemingly from thin air. "Where are you hurt?" she demanded, her voice sharp with concern. "Let's see it." She slanted an irritated glance at Ari. "Why didn't you tell me?"

Ari raised her hands in surrender. "Samara promised to visit medical as soon as she had time."

Stella gestured impatiently at me. I stood with a wince and dropped my pants. I knew better than to argue with Stella when she was on a mission. She inspected the bandage on my thigh, ran the scanner over my leg, and made various noncommittal noises before she finally conceded, "It's decent. For now."

She pulled an injector and fitted it with a vial—Stella was like a walking medicine chest. I stopped her before she pressed it against my skin. "I need to be able to think clearly," I said. "I'll deal with the pain."

She rolled her eyes at me. "I *do* know what I'm doing."

I gestured her on. Stella pressed the injector below my injury and pulled the trigger. After she helped me back into my chair, she sat down next to Ari and mock glared at her. "This is just the most convenient seat. I'm still mad at you for hiding Samara's injury."

Ari grinned and tugged Stella close. Stella made a pretense of fighting the pull, then melted into Ari's side. "You know how she is," Ari said, "as stubborn as a goat."

They both nodded knowingly at me while I pretended ignorance.

The pain in my thigh faded, but I didn't notice any of the drowsy, disconnected feeling I'd had before. "It seems you have the good drugs," I said to Stella.

"Of course," she agreed with a wink. Her expression turned serious. "Where is the Emperor?"

"He's getting cleaned up," Ari said. She snickered and continued, "You should've seen Samara's face when he mentioned the shower."

I kept my expression bland. It fooled neither of them, but I was saved from further teasing by the sound of the bedroom door opening.

"Samara, would you mind helping me for a second, please?" Valentin asked.

"Sure," I said. When I stood, my thigh ached but no longer felt like it might fall off. I made a mental note to stock *Invictia* with whatever Stella had given me.

I stepped into the short hallway leading to the bedrooms and nearly fell on my face. Valentin stood in the doorway of the far bedroom, wearing drawstring pants slung low around his lean hips and no shirt.

I somehow continued moving toward him without tripping.

His dark, damp hair fell over his forehead. He hadn't shaved, so dark stubble shadowed his jaw. My gaze kept drifting lower. A vast swath of golden skin and hard muscles was on display. Flat chest, defined abs, and those sexy v-shaped muscles that directed my eyes downward, only to be thwarted at the last minute by his pants.

There was no way that he hadn't caught me checking him out, so I just shrugged and rolled with it. "What kind of help do you need that doesn't require a shirt?"

I heard Ari snort from the living room.

"I need you to remove the bandage from my back," he said, his voice a little deeper than usual. "I can't reach it, and it's driving me crazy."

"Would you like Stella to look at it? She's a doctor."

Valentin was already shaking his head before I finished speaking. "No, I don't need a doctor. I would prefer you to do it. Please," he said softly.

"Okay, turn around," I said.

He obeyed. There were red spots above and below the elastomer bandage where he'd irritated his skin trying to reach it. I used my fingernail to peel up one edge. "Fast or slow?" I asked.

He grinned at me over his shoulder. "Fast."

"This is going to hurt," I warned. I gripped the edge of the bandage with my right hand and pressed my left hand against his shoulder for leverage. "On three. One—" I ripped the bandage off.

Once he finished cursing, he glared at me. "You need to learn how to count," he growled.

"The bandage is off, isn't it? Come on, I'll clean up the adhesive for you."

As I wiped the alcohol pad carefully around his wound, I was impressed by the amount of healing that had happened in just a day. The wound looked at least a week old, maybe more. It was healed enough that it didn't even need a gauze cover.

I pressed my fingers to his skin, checking for any remaining tackiness. "You're good to go," I said.

Valentin turned to face me, putting me entirely too close to the expanse of his chest. I pulled my gaze up. The bruising around his eye was already starting to fade. Thanks to a glance in the mirror, I knew mine was still turning a deeper shade of purple. Faster healing must be nice.

"Thank you," he said.

"You're welcome. Meet us in the living room when you're ready."

He nodded. I stepped away from temptation before I could do something I might not regret—at least for a while.

———

IN THE LIVING ROOM, Stella and Ari shot me identical sly glances from the couch. "I don't want to hear it," I said when Ari opened her mouth. I settled into the same chair I'd been in before.

Stella ignored me. "Was it a *hard* problem to solve?" she asked with a politely inquiring expression. "Is that why it took so long?"

Ari cracked up. Stella tried to keep it together but when I rolled my eyes at her, she lost it and started snickering.

"You two are the worst," I said without heat.

"You know you love us," Stella replied with a smile.

Valentin padded into the room on bare feet. He'd put on a shirt that stretched nicely across his chest, hinting at the muscles underneath.

Stella and Ari turned serious, their earlier playfulness gone. Valentin continued to the chair next to mine as if he didn't notice the sudden tension in the air.

"Valentin, meet Stella Mueller, my head of medical," I said. "Stella, meet Emperor Valentin Kos."

"A pleasure, I'm sure," Stella murmured coolly.

Valentin nodded. "Likewise."

I decided to dive right in. "Everyone saw the response from the Kos Empire I forwarded you?" At their nods, I continued, "Valentin, is this what you were expecting?"

He glanced at Stella and Ari.

"They are my closest advisors," I said. "They'll hear everything you tell me whether or not they're here, so let's not waste my time by making me repeat it."

"I want you all to swear what I am going to tell you will not leave this room," he said at last.

"Is it going to affect my people?"

"No," he said.

"Then I swear I will not share what you tell us with anyone outside this room." Stella agreed easily enough, but Ari's mouth set. I glared at her until she finally repeated the oath.

"In the Kos Empire, the Emperor has the final say in all matters, but the Emperor's advisors wield a great deal of power on their own. Needless to say, very few of them were pleased when they read Father's will and found out I was the named heir instead of my older brother Nikolas."

"Why *were* you named heir?" Ari asked.

"Father died before he could explain his choice," Valentin said with a shrug.

"You must have some idea," Ari persisted.

"Of course," Valentin said easily, "but it isn't relevant to this conversation. My advisors want me dead because I threaten their power. Your involvement was too convenient for them to pass up."

"But the response came from a generic account. Anyone could have sent it. How is that helpful?"

"I can track it," he said. "It won't get me specifics, but it's a place to start." He caught my gaze. "If this were real, if you sent the ransom request and they came back with a demand for my death, what would you have done?"

I stared at him while I weighed my words. "I don't know," I

said at last. "It's easy to take the moral high ground when it's just a theoretical, but ten million credits would buy a lot of food."

"Would you truly kill me to save your people?" Valentin asked.

I couldn't read his expression, so I answered him honestly. "In cold blood? No. My soul doesn't need any more stains. But I would absolutely play you and your advisors against each other, trying to get as much money as possible."

Valentin grinned at me. "Let's do that, then. If you can get a payment, it'll help narrow down who's involved."

"I get to keep anything I get from your advisors, in addition to the money you still owe me," I said.

"You can keep half," Valentin replied immediately.

Stella scoffed. "Do you value your allies so little? Without Samara's help, your plan goes nowhere."

"You can keep whatever they give you, but half of the value will be deducted from the amount I owe you."

"I do understand math, and while I would love for them to give me more than seven million up front to make that deal worth my while, I doubt they are going to. Whatever they are stupid enough to hand over, I keep. Our existing deal remains as is."

"You can keep the money, as long as you agree to make a good faith effort to negotiate a peace treaty with me after this is over."

Ari made a furious sound of protest but I sliced her a silencing glare. "I agree I will make a good faith effort, but as you can see, my council is highly unlikely to accept a treaty without extremely favorable conditions. I suggested the idea months ago and they shot me down."

"Fair enough," Valentin said.

He held out his hand and we shook on it. I could *feel* Ari glaring daggers into the side of my head, but money was money and we needed more of it. I expected the peace treaty to fall through, but I'd been honest when I made the agreement. Valentin couldn't say that he wasn't warned.

We argued over the exact wording of the response for long

enough that I started struggling to keep my eyes open. I was going on three days of too little sleep and no longer had the patience for diplomacy.

It was supposed to be my response, so I finally just responded how I actually would've. I asked for half of the money to be deposited in a secure drop account, with the rest payable on proof of Valentin's death.

Ari and Stella offered to stay, but I waved them off. If Valentin tried to murder me in my sleep, he'd find I was harder to kill than I looked, even bone-weary. I showed them to the door, then trudged to the second bedroom to strip a blanket and pillow from the bed.

"What are you doing?" Valentin asked from the door.

"Sleeping on the couch," I said without turning around.

"Why?"

"Because if I get into this bed, I'm going to pass out. I won't insult you by curling up in front of the door, but I want to know if you're up and moving."

"You could always sleep with me," Valentin said. My head snapped around so quickly that he held his hands up defensively. "Sleep only," he clarified. "The bed is big enough and you would know if I moved."

If temptation had a mortal form, it would look just like Valentin Kos. I wavered for a second, before reason reasserted itself. "I appreciate the offer, but the couch is fine," I said. I grabbed a pillow and moved toward the door.

He stood his ground. "I promise I'll keep my hands to myself," he said.

"It's not you I'm worried about," I said under my breath.

Unfortunately, he caught it and grinned at me before his expression turned serious. "You're injured and exhausted. You need a good night's rest."

"I can sleep anywhere," I said. "Stop arguing so I can get to it."

Valentin stepped back. I brushed past him and turned toward

the living room. I wrapped myself in the blanket and tried to get comfy on the couch. It was a few centimeters too small, even for my short height.

I gave up and moved to the floor. The rug helped a little, but it would still be an uncomfortable night. However, I'd slept in far worse conditions.

I had just gotten settled on my left side when Valentin stepped into the living room carrying a blanket and pillow.

"What are you doing?" I asked.

"I'm not going to sleep in a bed while you're on the floor."

"You could always sleep on the floor in your room," I said.

Valentin flashed me a grin, then wrapped himself in his blanket and lay down less than a meter away. Nervous energy flooded my system as I realized that I could reach out an arm and touch him.

Valentin turned onto his side and caught me staring at him. I hadn't taken out my contacts, so his face was visible in the greenish gray of my night vision.

"I thought you were exhausted," he said softly.

"I was," I agreed. "I'm not used to sleeping with someone so close."

"No brothers or sisters when you were growing up?"

"No," I said. "I always wanted a little brother, but it's probably for the best that I didn't get my wish." My early life had been bleak. I preferred not to think about it.

Valentin caught my closed expression and didn't press. "My brother and I never got along, even though he's only a year older. Now I wonder if he suspected even then."

"Suspected what?"

He searched my face for a long moment before he spoke. "Nikolas is my half-brother," Valentin said quietly. "We share the same mother, but not the same father."

The ramifications of that statement took a few seconds to sink in, but when they did, my eyes widened. "He's illegitimate? How do you know?"

"After Father changed the line of succession, I had suspicions. I searched Father's old files and found enough vague references to confront Mother. She confessed. A DNA test would prove it."

"Did your father know the whole time?" I asked carefully, aware that I might be probing too deep into a wound that still bled.

Valentin sighed and rolled over onto his back. "Father knew," he told the ceiling. "He claimed Nikolas because he loved Mother and didn't want to see her shamed, but on his deathbed, he must've decided he wouldn't put an illegitimate son on the throne. I haven't announced it because I love my mother and stars know Father was no saint."

"Does anyone else know? Does *Nikolas*?"

Valentin turned his head toward me, his expression stark. "Mother told Nikolas after Father's death. She thought it would help him understand Father's decision. Nikolas did not take it well," he said drily.

If you spent your whole life thinking you were the Emperor's son, destined to be the next Emperor, and then it turned out you were secretly illegitimate, I could see how that would be a tough blow. No wonder Nikolas wanted Valentin dead.

"I'm sorry," I said. I reached across the distance separating us and squeezed his upper arm. Words were nice, but sometimes you just needed physical comfort to know that another person was there and cared.

He tensed. I pulled back, afraid I'd overstepped. After a second, he caught my hand in a gentle grip. I forced myself to stay relaxed. I hadn't been kidding about not being used to sleeping so close. Normally when I was lying this close to a man, sleeping was the last thing on our minds.

I promptly shut down that line of thought before it could get off the ground.

"Thank you," Valentin murmured.

"You're welcome," I whispered back.

Valentin's breathing slowly changed until it was deep and even. I relaxed into the rhythm. I thought his closeness would keep me awake, but my body was far too tired to care. I sank into sleep like an anchor.

———

FOR THE SECOND time in as many days, I awoke to alarms. My eyes felt leaden, like I'd barely closed them. A body moved next to me and my eyes popped open to an unfamiliar room.

Right, I was in the living room of the guest suite with Valentin. Sometime in the night, I'd crossed the distance separating us. I was pressed up against his side through layers of blankets.

"Why is the alarm going off?" Valentin mumbled. "Is this normal?"

I sat up and blinked. Neural links were coming in faster than I could answer them. I recognized Ari's signature and opened the link.

What's going on? I growled without moving. I wasn't getting up if this was Ari's idea of a fun time for a training exercise.

A quartet of warships just tunneled on top of us—a battle cruiser, a destroyer, and two corvettes. They have at least a squadron of fighters in the air and they're shooting anything that moves. They've already taken out most of our outer defenses. Two platoons are on the ground. The ships are unflagged, but the soldiers are wearing what looks like Kos armor. Watch your back with the Emperor.

That woke me up. *Evacuate the civilians now,* I sent through the link. *Tell them to head for the tunnels. Do not engage the enemy troops unless it's to get people to the evac zone. We'll hold the tunnel doors open as long as we can. I will deal with Valentin.*

Valentin sat up. "What's happening?"

"I told you I would kill you if you betrayed me," I said. My voice sounded eerily calm to my own ears. "You have ten seconds to explain why Kos soldiers are attacking my city."

Valentin blinked at me as the alarm tone changed to the tunnel evacuation cadence. He held up his hands. "I swear I didn't order an attack," he said. "Are the ships broadcasting Kos allegiance?"

"No, but the soldiers are wearing Kos armor."

His eyes went distant before they narrowed. "Son of a *bitch*," he growled vehemently. "Those aren't my troops, but they *are* wearing prototype Kos armor."

I realized that he had tapped into our surveillance video as easily as if it were broadcast on an open com. I needed to figure out how his neural ability worked and if there was any way to block it, but right now we had more immediate problems.

Fury laced his voice as he continued, "Kos scientists spent years developing that armor. It was supposed to be top secret, in testing only for our elite squads, not on two fucking platoons of Quint Confederacy mercenaries."

"You think these are Quint soldiers? How did they get their hands on your armor? Your advisors?"

"They are definitely Quint. I don't know how they got our armor, but I'm going to find out," he said, his voice deadly.

"Get up," I said. "We have to evacuate."

With fighters in the air it would be suicide to launch evac ships from the main base. We had a secondary launch point five kilometers away via tunnel, but not enough ships for everyone. It would be chaos.

"I thought you said you could hold off Commander Adams?" Valentin asked while he pulled on his boots.

"We could, but he brought backup, and we can't hold against four ships. If you have a fleet within range, call them in. Otherwise, you're going to be evacuating with us."

Valentin says the troops are Quint, but they're wearing prototype Kos armor. I don't think he's lying. I told Ari as I hustled Valentin from the suite.

97

Whoever they are, they are running silent, Ari said. *Our attempts to hail them have been ignored.*

I ran for my quarters, Valentin on my heels. Inside, I slammed open the doors to my personal armory and started pulling out gear. I wrapped a utility belt around my waist and strapped a plasma pistol on each hip. I secured a combat knife on my right flank. A dozen extra magazines filled with lethal, highly illegal armor-piercing plasma rounds went in a pouch on my left flank.

I did not plan to take prisoners.

I handed Valentin a plasma pistol, a holster, and three extra magazines. "I'm trusting you."

He nodded solemnly, then slung the holster around his waist. "I have a battle fleet within range, but your communication satellite is terrible. By the time they get the message, they should've already detected the Quint ships."

"Send it anyway," I said. "We'll hold as long as we can, but we are not equipped for a full-scale attack. How did they get ships here so quickly?"

"They must've been nearby. This sector is usually pretty quiet, but we've had a few skirmishes with Quint ships within tunneling distance of Trigon Three."

We just had to hold long enough for the Kos fleet to show up. The fact that we needed rescue annoyed me, but I wasn't stupid enough to turn down help with enemies standing on my doorstep.

I slung a compact plasma rifle over my shoulder and closed the armory. I headed for the door. "Let's go."

Where are you? I asked Ari across the link.

I'm headed for the market, she said, sounding breathless. *I've got a squad and Malcolm has a squad. The rest are still trickling in. We're setting up blockades in the western hallway. I'm sending Malcolm to you.*

No, I countered. *Keep him there. I have Valentin. We'll check the rooms on this side, then make our way over. Keep the civilians safe. Link me again if things change.* I closed the neural link before she could protest.

From the air looking down, the underground part of Arx was roughly T-shaped. Arx's main hallway was the top of the T and ran east-west. The shorter southern hallway was the T's base. The surface-level entrance was located where the two hallways met.

The market, primary hangar, and most of the residences branched off the main hallway west of the entrance. The evacuation tunnel started at the far western end of the main hallway.

Besides my quarters and the guest suite, the eastern half of Arx included various storage and utility rooms, the secondary hangar, and the mess hall. The southern hallway led to the large maintenance areas.

Unfortunately, because we were on the east side, Valentin and I were on our own until we hit the market.

I took the stairs down two at a time while I pulled up the base's outside vid feeds. Sure enough, at least fifty soldiers in full combat armor were creeping across the base directly toward the main entrance. The entrance was not obvious from looking at the above-ground base layout, even from the air—they'd gotten their hands on the plans.

They were not being bombarded by plasma pulses, so they must've taken out the automated turrets, which meant they had an open path to the door. We needed to haul ass.

13

The main hallway echoed with the shrill cadence of the evacuation alarm. All of the fire doors were closed, narrowing my view to a small sliver of the long hallway. Around us, nothing moved. Valentin followed as I did a quick sweep of the storage and utility rooms, but anyone who had been over here had already cleared out.

We ran toward the center of the base. I burst through a set of fire doors with Valentin just behind me on my right. Ahead of us, Eddie Tarlowski, the head chef, emerged from the mess hall with a plasma pistol in his right hand and a huge kitchen knife in his mechanical left hand.

He paused when he saw us running toward him. "Boss, what's going on?" he yelled.

I slowed down to a jog as we caught up to him and he fell in on my left. "The Quint Empire is attacking. We're evacuating through the western tunnels. Why are you here?"

"Couldn't sleep," he said with a half shrug. "Decided to get started on the day. Then the alarms went off. Thought it might be a drill, so I put the food away. Brought the knife in case it wasn't."

"It's not a drill," I said as I checked on the vids. The soldiers outside had nearly made it to the main door. The door was two levels up, but the entryway was a three-story open atrium. Once the door was breached, we wouldn't have any cover. They could pick us off from the balcony.

"Come on," I ordered. "We have to get past the entrance before they blow the door."

I sped up and Eddie and Valentin easily paced me. My thigh burned with a distant pain, but whatever drugs Stella had given me were *awesome*. I'd likely pay for it later, but for now, I'd take it.

The doors to the atrium loomed just ahead. On the security vid, soldiers stuck explosives to the main entrance door. The timing would be dangerously close.

We burst into the atrium just as the soldiers pulled away from the door. "Move!" I shouted. I dashed into a sprint. Eddie and Valentin easily kept pace, proving they both had speed augments.

The fire doors on the west side of the atrium were open and I could see all the way to the market, where a makeshift barricade made out of what looked like hull shielding blocked the hall just behind an open set of doors. Ari stood in the middle of the havoc, shouting orders.

We had barely cleared the first set of doors into the western hallway when the building shook with an explosion. Two seconds later, I heard the distinctive sound of grenades hitting the atrium steps.

Valentin tackled me to the ground. The rifle across my back dug in painfully as he covered me with his body. Eddie kept running. Behind us, the atrium exploded into a fury of sound and light. At least our unwelcome guests were only using stun grenades. Valentin pulled me up and pushed me in front of him. We bolted for the barricade.

Once we were safely behind cover, Ari looked me over, checking for injuries. "I'm glad you made it," she said.

"Me, too. What's the situation?"

"I've got most of our soldiers helping the civilians evacuate.

Imogen took a squad to lead the way to the ships, just in case they meet resistance on the way. We'll hold here as long as we can, then close and blockade the doors to give us time to fall back."

"The Quint soldiers went straight for the entrance," I said. "They must have a map."

Ari nodded. She was linked in to the security feed, too.

"They're here for Valentin, but I embarrassed Commander Adams, so they'd be plenty happy to grab me as well," I said. "Valentin has a battle fleet within range, so we need to hold until they arrive."

"And if they don't arrive?" Ari asked with a frown.

"We'll cross that canyon when we get there," I said. "For now, we focus on getting the civilians into the tunnels and holding the line."

Deeper in the market, Stella and two of her nurses stood beside three huge duffels emblazoned with red crosses. She'd cleaned out medical in preparation for casualties.

I dearly hoped it wouldn't come to that.

I hunkered down behind the barricade, Valentin beside me. The hallway to the atrium was clear. I checked the outside video. Soldiers were entering the building in teams of four. They crept down the east stairs, sweeping for targets.

Outside, a team launched a Ghost miniature surveillance drone. Nearly silent, the drone was smaller across than a typical dinner plate and only ten centimeters tall.

I turned to Valentin. "They have a Ghost. Stay out of sight."

Valentin's jaw clenched, but he nodded.

The drone pilot's teammates covered him as he directed the drone inside. In the atrium, both the east and south tunnel doors were closed, so the drone headed our way. Yay.

Ari caught my arm before I could stand up. "You should stay hidden," she said.

"Probably," I agreed. "But it is my responsibility."

I stood from behind the barricade before she could argue

further. I drew my plasma pistol as the drone came into view. "I am Queen Samara Rani. This wing contains civilians, including children. If you continue, we will be forced to defend ourselves."

The drone paused. I mentally watched the security feed as the pilot relayed the information. His commander held up a hand.

"Samara Rani, we meet again," Commander Adams said, his voice tinny from the drone's speaker.

"Commander Adams, I don't see you on the ground, so you must be hiding in your ship. Afraid to face me when I'm not chained to a chair?"

I kept an eye on the vid of the inside soldiers. I'd long ago learned to split my focus, and I wouldn't put it past them to use the drone as a distraction to get a shot at me.

It's what I would've done if I were in their place.

Commander Adams laughed. "It's cute that you think you're a threat. Give me the Emperor and I won't destroy your city."

"Okay," I agreed easily. Valentin tensed beside me. "But you have to come down and get him yourself."

"Show me proof that he's there."

"No can do, I'm afraid. He's confined and your soldiers have me pinned down here." The longer I could keep him talking, the more time my people had to evacuate.

Behind the drone, two teams of four crossed the doorway. I tensed to dodge behind cover but they crossed without taking a potshot at me. Leaving cover was ballsy, though at this distance a plasma pistol with standard ammo wasn't a serious threat with them in full-body combat armor—but they didn't know that I wasn't using standard ammo.

I gritted my teeth and let the soldiers pass unscathed.

"Adams, if your people keep entering my home, I'm going to start shooting at them. Are you coming down, or are you going to continue leading from the back while your soldiers take all the risk?"

"A leader leads while the soldiers soldier. You would know that if you led anything more than a bunch of criminals and vagabonds."

"You tell yourself that, but cowardice by any other name is still cowardice," I taunted.

"I'm going to enjoy bringing you and your people to heel like the dogs that you are, you little—"

Before he could complete that sentence, I pulled my pistol up, aimed for a weak spot in the drone's armor plating, and squeezed the trigger. The pulse tore through the drone's armor and shredded the internals. The fuel exploded in a flash of light and sent shrapnel skidding down the hallway, then the drone dropped to the ground, dead.

Well, that got someone's attention.

All of the soldiers in the atrium froze, then two teams moved down the stairs with swift efficiency and stacked against the entrance to our hallway. I edged back until I was mostly behind the makeshift barricade and watched as the lead soldier peeked around the corner for a heartbeat before ducking back into cover.

There was a very thin line between brave and stupid, and I wanted to stay on the right side of it. Quint had a few well-known sharpshooters and while I didn't know they were out there right now, I didn't know they *weren't*, either. I moved farther into cover.

"Nice shot," Valentin said when I crouched down beside him.

"Thanks," I said. It wasn't the first Ghost I'd shot down and hopefully it wouldn't be the last.

"How close are we to having everyone in the tunnels?" I asked Ari.

"Not close enough," she muttered.

"Have you heard anything from your fleet?" I asked Valentin.

He silently shook his head.

An arm appeared at the soldiers' end of the tunnel and slid a small puck-like object down the hallway toward us. A blink later, the atrium disappeared and my reflection stared back at me, mostly hidden behind the barricade.

It was one of the better active camouflage units I'd seen. The technology was typically used to hide large vehicles by taking a video from behind the vehicle and displaying it on the front, effectively rendering the vehicle invisible. In this case, they'd flipped the camera around. When I shifted slightly, there was no visible lag between my movement and the reflection—it looked just like a mirror.

I checked the internal security video. Three teams were positioned outside the southern hallway and three more teams were outside the eastern hallway.

Four teams waited at the entrance to our hallway. The only consolation was if they tried to enter, they would have no cover. It would be like shooting fish in a barrel, something they very well knew.

I settled in to wait for Quint to make the first move. Waiting would let them get more soldiers on the ground, but it also gave my civilians more time to evacuate.

And maybe it would give Valentin's fleet enough time to arrive.

———

IT HAD BEEN ten minutes and Quint still hadn't attacked. I shifted to prevent my legs from cramping, the only fidgeting I allowed myself. What were they waiting for?

More Rogue Coalition soldiers had arrived from the barracks. We now had superior numbers to the Quint troops on the ground, but the hallway worked against us. The narrow entrance meant only a small fraction of our troops would have a clear line of fire.

"Where's our next fallback point?" I asked. Ari had experience planning battle strategies. I had experience flying solo, so I left the details to her.

The market sprawled to our north. It provided plenty of cover, but any troops stationed there would be cut off from quick escape to the tunnels. They would have to go up and around through the main hangar—which might be an attack point by then.

Ari must've shared my concerns because she said, "On the other side of the market, at the hallway to the barracks. Soldiers are setting up a blockade, but we won't be able to hold it long. It's mostly to buy us time to get the last of the civilians out."

The tunnel entrance was twenty meters past that hallway intersection. If we lost the intersection, anyone left in the residential part of the base would be unable to escape. We needed to hold it as long as possible.

Movement in the security videos caught my attention. A troop transport landed near the base's main entrance and another platoon of soldiers poured out.

The soldiers in the atrium sprang into action. They stacked in single-file lines outside of each hallway. At some unseen signal, they simultaneously lowered the visors on their combat helmets. Two seconds later, every single soldier in the atrium shimmered and disappeared.

Holy shit, Kos had perfected the personal camouflage on their combat armor and now Quint benefited from their prototypes. Rumors had been rampant for years but I'd never seen any proof.

Ari and I shared an incredulous look before the fire doors in front of us slammed closed. Ari was obviously still linked to the security system that controlled the doors.

"Bar the door!" she shouted.

Five soldiers picked up a long metal beam and wedged it into the hooks that had been welded to the back of the doors. Once they were clear, a dozen soldiers heaved the makeshift barricade forward into the door. It wouldn't hold forever, but it would slow down the Quint Confederacy soldiers.

"Fall back!" Ari commanded. She motioned Stella and her nurses ahead of the soldiers.

Once most of the soldiers had cleared out, I rounded on Valentin. "Why the fuck didn't you tell me that the prototype armor had active camouflage?" I hissed, trying to keep my voice down.

Valentin scowled. "I had hoped my fleet would arrive and make the point moot. It took us two decades to perfect that technology; I'm not used to just telling everyone I meet about it."

Anger turned my vision red. I took a deep breath before I throttled him. "Any other secrets I should know about before I risk my people defending your ass from a host of Quint soldiers?"

His jaw clenched, but he said, "Even with the camouflage active, the armor shows up in thermal views, including thermal vision augments."

Once again, movement pulled my attention back to the security video. In the atrium, the doors to all three hallways opened at once but none of the soldiers showed up on the video. It was creepy as hell.

Ari did a final sweep of the area. "Time to go," she said.

I turned to her. "The soldiers show up on thermal. Find every soldier with augments."

She nodded, then we jogged for the next barricade. We'd barely made it when a deafening explosion echoed down the hallway. The Quint soldiers were not wasting any time, the bastards.

The small stream of civilians had frozen in place. "MOVE!" I shouted. "Get to the tunnel *now!*"

They broke and ran, but they weren't trampling each other, so I let them run. We needed them in the tunnel ten minutes ago. The stream slowed until only the occasional straggler hurried through.

"I want everyone out of the barracks and every civilian in the tunnel in the next two minutes!" Ari shouted at her troops. "Lorenzo and Montgomery, take a team each and make it happen!" Two soldiers saluted, gathered three more soldiers each, then headed for the residential section at a run.

The remaining soldiers shoved additional shielding across the hallway. Overall, this blockade was smaller. The lower half looked like hull shielding again, but most of the height was achieved by using overlapping riot shields. They would deflect some distance shots, but once the Quint soldiers closed on us they would offer less protection.

Ari kept a squad of eight with us and sent everyone else, including Stella and her nurses, to wait in the tunnel. We would hold here until everyone was out of the barracks, then retreat down the hallway until we were safely behind the tunnel's blast door.

I tried to send Valentin into safety, but he smiled grimly at me and planted himself behind the barricade. I had three point five million reasons to keep him safe, but I didn't have an electroshock pistol. Short of knocking him out, he wasn't moving.

I couched down beside him where I had a clear shot at the door through a gap in the riot shields. I did a final check of my plasma rifle, then settled down to wait. The seconds ticked by with agonizing slowness. I focused on breathing and blocked out the fidgeting soldiers around me.

Ari crouched down on the other side of me and tilted her head. "They're coming," she said quietly. "You should head to the tunnel."

"Did you really think that would work?" I asked.

"No, but I had to try," she said. "He's not leaving, either?"

"No," Valentin said at the same time I said, "Apparently not."

Ari shook her head at us but didn't argue. She turned to the gathered soldiers and shouted, "We will hold this line until Lorenzo and Montgomery return! Do not let me down! Do not let your Queen down!"

Our soldiers roared their assent.

"The Quint soldiers will seem invisible, but trust your spotter. If your spotter is blind, then suppressive fire is the name of the game. Now let's show these assholes who they're fucking with!"

The soldiers roared again.

Then there was no time for talking. The fire doors ten meters in front of us burst open and stayed that way, wedged open by part of our own damn barricade from the market. So much for shooting fish in a barrel.

The barricade crept toward us, pushed by invisible hands.

I listened as the spotters started giving targets and our soldiers opened fire. The plasma pistol in Valentin's hands spat pulses as he aimed at invisible targets. Ari moved up and down the line, giving orders. The nearest spotter said, "Center, ten cm left of the high point."

I fired off two quick rounds and red mist sprayed out from a still invisible body. I couldn't even tell what I'd hit, but Quint reacted with a wall of plasma fire.

"Down," Ari yelled. Pulses tore into the riot shields above us and left behind the acrid stench of hot metal. A couple of pulses punched through and a Coalition soldier screamed.

What I wouldn't give to be able to use a bucket of grenades right now. But in an enclosed area like this, I'd be just as likely to take out my own soldiers. The Quint troops must've decided the same thing.

The world narrowed. *Shoot. Duck. Reposition.* Repeat.

We missed more often than we hit, and the Quint barricade crept steadily closer. A pulse clipped the top of my left shoulder, centimeters from my face. I repositioned again, but there was nowhere to go. In minutes we'd be overrun.

"The barracks are clear! Team one, fall back and support! Team two, suppressive fire!" Ari shouted over the noise of battle.

Half of our soldiers disengaged and ran bent over toward the tunnel entrance while the rest of us put enough pulses in the air to keep the Quint troops from firing at them. I was down to a single extra magazine for my rifle. I slammed it home and prayed it would be enough.

"Team two, fall back! Stay low against the wall," Ari said.

"But—" a male voice started.

"That's an order, soldier!"

The soldiers ran for the tunnel. Ari, Valentin, and I swept the Quint barricade with plasma fire. Pulses whistled overhead from behind as our teams in the tunnel shot at the Quint soldiers over our heads.

Ari pulled two grenades.

"Planning to go down in a blaze of glory?" I asked.

"They're smoke. When I toss them, grab a shield, hold it behind you, and run like hell." She cut me off before I could protest. "I'll be right beside you. Valentin, you're in front of us. Stay close to the wall so our soldiers don't shoot you."

She pulled the pin and tossed the first grenade over the barricade. Thick white smoke billowed up. She pulled the pin of the second grenade and tossed it a meter toward the tunnel entrance. More smoke billowed until I could barely see.

Plasma pulses still flew overhead. We moved to the edge of the barricade, grabbed a riot shield each, and ran for the tunnel door. Twenty meters had never seemed so far.

Valentin looked back to check on us, and Ari yelled at him, "Run faster, asshole! I'm not dying because of you."

A pulse grazed me just below my existing thigh wound and stars exploded in my vision. I gritted my teeth and forged on. Four meters from the tunnel entrance, Ari went down. "Leave me!" she shouted.

I swung my shield around and backtracked two steps. Valentin turned and shot over our heads as I pulled Ari to her feet. I would *not* leave my best friend to be murdered by the soldiers I'd called down upon us.

Her left calf was a mangled mess. I looped my right arm through the middle shield handle and wrapped it around her back, then pulled her left arm over my shoulder and half-carried her. My right leg burned with the heat of the sun, but we hobbled for the tunnel entrance.

Valentin started to come back for us, but I waved him off. He retreated toward the tunnel door, shooting over Ari's shoulder.

Plasma fire sparked and sizzled all around us. From our front, Coalition soldiers laid down suppressive fire as they tried to avoid us while shooting targets they couldn't see. Behind us, the Quint soldiers did their best to kill us before we made it to safety.

Ari and I were just a meter away from the door when white-hot pain blasted through my back and out my left side. Numbness immediately followed. I didn't need to look to know it was a devastating wound.

Someone shouted, but the world was strangely muted. I summoned the last of my reserves and heaved us through the door opening, then collapsed. I took Ari down with me. I didn't feel the impact, but I did hear the reassuring sound of the heavy blast doors closing. I breathed out a sigh of relief. The Quint soldiers would need a mountain of explosives to make it through. My people would be long gone by then.

Someone rolled me over and tore off my shirt. Stella's face appeared above me, wan and wavy. I blinked as her lips moved. She rolled me onto my right side and clamped something hard and heavy around my left side that burned like acid and compressed my chest. I tried to wiggle away, but my body failed to respond to my commands.

I blinked, and I was on a stretcher, being carried by two soldiers. Valentin scowled down at me and said something I didn't catch. My side hurt. Breathing hurt. Everything hurt.

Another blink and the white walls of medical blinded me. Were we still in Arx? Had we failed after all?

Ari leaned over me. Her face was too pale, and her mouth was pinched the way that it did when she was unspeakably upset. She radiated pure, ferocious determination. "Do. Not. Die," she commanded. "I forbid it." She continued but her voice faded out as my vision edged in black.

I blinked, but this time my eyelids were too heavy to open.

14

After a week in a med chamber, I was ready to escape—a week in a med chamber was an *eon*. I'd been unconscious for most of it and only remembered brief snatches of time.

The auto-doc had done its job well. I'd woken up yesterday nearly healed. Despite my protests, Stella had put me under for another day, but that ended now.

I needed *out*.

Ari had given me brief updates in the short periods I had been awake. Her leg had healed in less than a day—a day she had been awake and working—but she had deflected my questions with an admonishment to rest. And I couldn't wrangle the rest of the information out of her if I remained trapped in medical.

"Twelve more hours would do you good," Stella grumbled from the other side of the clear med chamber hood. "You nearly died a few days ago. If I hadn't had the trauma-doc, you would've." She scowled as she scrolled through my medical diagnostics.

I doubted she could find anything in the report that would prevent me from escaping. Truth be told, I felt awesome. Both my thigh and side were completely healed, covered over in smooth skin without even a scar as a reminder.

Stella sighed in defeat. "If I let you out, I want your word that you won't lift anything heavier than a kilogram for the next three days." I started to protest and she cut me off. "I will knock you out again if I have to," she said with a deadly serious gleam in her eye.

I knew when to accept gracious defeat. "I won't lift anything heavier than a kilogram for three days," I promised.

"Okay, get up, shower, and get dressed while I find Ari. She'll be keeping you honest," she said. She motioned toward the back of the room. "Shower's the door on the right."

I nodded meekly. Beneath the scowls and grumbles, Stella was too pale, her face drawn. According to Ari, she'd been up constantly the first few days, monitoring my condition and tweaking the auto-doc's settings. As soon as I'd seen her face, I'd known just how close to death I'd skated.

Stella left. The med chamber hood swung open, and I sat up with a grimace. Despite the electrical stimulation the chamber used to prevent muscle atrophy, I felt stiff and sore.

I swung my legs over the side and eased up to standing. I expected my right thigh to hurt, but other than the faint tremble of unused muscles, I felt great. It was going to be really hard to remember my promise, which was probably why Stella decided to attach Ari to my side.

A glance around revealed a dozen other med chambers, all thankfully empty. We were aboard *Asray*, the Rogue Coalition's only city-ship. The Coalition had started on this ship, back before we took over Trigon Three and Arx. It was our largest ship and the one with the best medical unit.

Now that I was up, I needed to see how much damage we'd taken, but first, I needed to get rid of the chemical and ozone stench from the med chamber. The smell clung to my skin and hair, reminding me of my previous stints in medical. I grabbed my clothes and headed for the tiny attached shower.

ARI WAS WAITING for me when I stepped out of the bathroom. "I see Stella wasn't joking about assigning me a babysitter," I said without heat. I smiled and pulled her into a hug. "I'm just glad I'm here for you to babysit."

She squeezed me tight. "Thanks for coming back for me. It was stupid and reckless, but I appreciate it."

"You're welcome," I said. I let her go and stepped back to eye her leg. "How's the calf?" I asked.

"It's healed. Thank the stars *Asray* has multiple med chambers. We made use of them, though you were the worst, by far."

"I know you've been holding out on me. Catch me up while we walk," I said. "I need to stretch my legs."

We left medical and turned right toward the heart of the ship and the midship port exit. I knew that *Asray* remained berthed in the emergency hangar. Now I needed to see Arx for myself.

"As you know, by the time we made it to the ships, the Kos fleet had arrived," Ari said. "We went ahead and put our injured in *Asray's* med chambers, just in case we needed to evacuate anyway. We had more than a dozen injured, but no casualties. You were by far the worst and too unstable to move back to Arx, so Stella and I stayed with you." She shook her head. "It could have been so much worse."

"Did Quint fight or run once Kos showed up?"

"They couldn't run because their stardrives weren't recharged. They fought, but for once Kos seemed prepared. All four Quint ships were destroyed." Ari's smile was sharp.

"Any Quint survivors?"

Her smile dimmed slightly. "An emergency shuttle tunneled away from *Deroga* before the Kos fighters could catch it. We assume Commander Adams was on board."

I frowned. Of course that cowardly little bastard would leave his soldiers to die while he escaped. I would have to deal with him soon or he'd be back to cause more trouble.

"What about Kos losses? Did Valentin survive?" I asked.

"The Kos fleet lost five fighters, but their main ships took only minor damage. And yes, Valentin survived unharmed," Ari said. "He left a couple of days ago with his last remaining ship."

Relief that he was alive warred with disappointment that he had departed without a word. I tried not to let the disappointment show, but Ari wasn't my best friend for nothing.

"He stayed until we were sure you would survive, but then he had to get back to his Empire," she said gently. "You would've done the same thing if you'd been gone that long."

I nodded in acknowledgment. "Did his advisors respond before he ran home and destroyed our chance at more money?"

Ari's eyes twinkled. "Yes, your little note netted us another five million credits. I bet they were furious when Valentin showed up just a few days later, looking no worse for wear."

I smiled as I imagined the advisors' reactions. Hopefully, Valentin was paying attention to who looked especially surprised or disgruntled.

"Has Quint declared war on us?"

"No, not yet," she said. "According to the news reports, Kos is giving them hell in the Phoenix sector. That seems to be keeping them busy for now."

"Let's hope they stay busy until they forget about us," I said. "Anything else?"

"The bulk of the Kos battle fleet stayed for twenty-four hours and then left. We're still picking up flickers on our sensors—they seem to be quietly patrolling the area. After everyone cleared out, we swept the entire compound with thermal imaging—every nook and cranny, every maintenance tunnel, everything. We didn't find any traps."

"How are repairs going? Are our defenses back online?"

"That's the other thing. Replacement turrets showed up before we even ordered them. And food and supplies keep arriving from Valentin."

Warmth warred with pride. Why was he sending supplies when all he owed me was credits? Unless, of course, he didn't plan to pay up, in which case I'd make him reassess that unfortunate decision.

"What's the general sentiment?" I asked.

"The civilians think you're a hero for getting us food," she said. "The soldiers think you're a hero for refusing to hide in safety when we were under attack. Spirits are generally very high."

I breathed out a silent sigh of relief. My people were safe for now. Everything else could be figured out later.

———

STELLA and I waited in the open-sided indoor transport while Ari put *Asray* into standby. "Thank you for saving my life," I said to Stella. "I know I'm a difficult patient, but I really do appreciate everything you do."

She shrugged off my words. "All of my favorite patients are difficult," she confided. "But that doesn't mean I won't bust your ass back to medical if I see you lifting anything even a gram over the limit. I have a scale and I'm not afraid to use it."

I laughed at the mental picture of her trailing me with a scale. She would do it, too. "I'll be on my best behavior," I told her honestly.

She muttered something under her breath that sounded very much like, "I'll believe it when I see it."

Ari returned, and Stella started up the transport for the quick trip to Arx. I reconnected to the net on the way and checked the news feed. The Kos Empire was celebrating the return of their Emperor, but there was no news of advisors' deaths. Had Valentin decided not to act after all? If so, I'd politely remind him of his advisors' treachery when I requested my second payment.

I checked my messages. I had four from the private account Valentin had used earlier. The most recent one was from this morning.

My heart kicked, but before I had a chance to open the message, we arrived at the market. The overhead panels twinkled with stars, and the gathered crowd cheered as I stepped out of the transport.

"You didn't really think I'd let those bastards kill me, did you?" I shouted. The crowd roared in approval.

Zita came forward, as happy as I'd ever seen her. "Come with me," she said. She pulled me along slowly. People kept stopping me to offer thanks or congratulations. Ari was right; despite the attack, everyone was in very good spirits.

I spotted Lily Dovers and a handsome young man standing snuggled together next to Lily's stern-faced father. Lily glowed with happiness. Apparently, Imogen had persuaded her to tell her father about the baby.

Zita sat me at the large metal table outside her bakery, then disappeared inside. Ari and Stella just grinned when I raised a questioning eyebrow at them.

The bakery door opened and Zita reappeared carrying an enormous tray of tiny, bite-sized desserts. She set the tray on the table. I could see the intricate flowers, swirls, and other decorations she'd created for each piece. My mouth watered.

"To the Queen's health!" Zita shouted.

"To the Queen's health!" the crowd shouted back. At this point I think they would've said anything to get one of her famous desserts, and I didn't blame them one bit.

Zita waved her hand at the tray, and I selected a golden-frosted square with a tiny crown of orange flowers. At Zita's nod, I took a bite. Spicy cake and sugary frosting exploded on my tongue, and I moaned in delight.

The crowd laughed, Zita beamed, and Ari nodded in approval.

Assistants brought out more trays, and the crowd joined me in the simple delight of food that did more than meet basic nutrition needs. A woman strummed a guitar while she and her husband sang a duet. Soon they were joined by more instruments.

The crowd's energy shifted, a dance floor was cleared, and the party began in earnest. Tonight would be a late night as people celebrated for the first time in months.

I mingled in the crowd for a few minutes, but curiosity was killing me. I wanted to read Valentin's messages in private. When everyone turned their attention to the dance floor, I slipped into the shadows and retreated to my quarters.

15

I settled behind the desk in my office, aware that I had a huge list of tasks that needed to be handled, not the least of which was putting our newfound wealth to work. But Valentin's messages beckoned, and I couldn't resist their pull.

I opened the first one, but before I'd even had a chance to read the first line, a video neural link from an unknown contact tickled the back of my mind. I hesitated, unsure if it was a weird coincidence.

Samara, please accept, Valentin's voice whispered through my head, so faint I almost thought I'd made it up. It should've been impossible, but I'd seen him do other impossible things.

I routed the link through my desktop terminal and accepted.

Valentin's face appeared on the vid screen in front of me. He'd shaved, showing off the smooth planes of his face. He wore a dark suit with a white shirt open at the collar. The casual elegance just added to his appeal.

"How are you?" he asked.

"I'm well enough that Stella let me out of the med chamber, but Ari is watching me like a hawk," I said. I could mentally link him, but the terminal's microphones would pick up my speech just as easily. "How about you? Your advisors giving you trouble?"

His lips quirked into a secret smile. "A half dozen of them have taken me aside to assure me that *they* are loyal, but they're not so sure about everyone else."

"Nikolas didn't take over while you were gone?" I asked.

"He wasn't in residence when I returned," Valentin said. The non-answer was telling. "There haven't been any outright attacks since I've been back."

It occurred to me that this video chat was the clearest I'd ever seen from our com system. The system usually wasn't good enough to handle a long-distance link, especially not a vid link. "How are you linking me? Are you nearby?"

Valentin grimaced, an expression I was beginning to learn meant he was about to tell me something I wasn't going to like.

"I am in Koan," he said. He gestured and the camera panned to show me his tastefully decorated office. "But I might've positioned a Kos communication satellite near you."

"You're spying on our communications?" I asked with a raised brow. "That's certainly presumptuous of you."

"No! The satellite is running dark. None of your traffic will go through it by default. I've used your com system," he said. "It's terrible. I wanted to be able to talk to you in real time. You owe me a peace treaty."

"I owe you a good-faith effort," I corrected. "Speaking of good faith, why are you sending us food and supplies? You *are* still planning to pay me, right?"

Valentin's expression shifted, turning serious. "I will transfer the second payment to your account today. Should I use the same account as before?"

I nodded.

"As for the food, I promised my plan wouldn't put your people at risk, but if I had gone directly home, Quint wouldn't have had a reason to attack you. That mistake is mine, and I owe you a debt. You need food and supplies; I have extra."

"Thank you," I said. The fact that he had a reason, that it wasn't just charity, soothed my ruffled pride.

"And it's to butter you up so I can get a better deal than a ten percent discount on those leadership classes I've heard you offer," he said with a smile.

That surprised a laugh out of me. "I'd be willing to go to a fifteen percent discount. That brings the price down from exorbitant to merely outrageous, but I'm sure you can afford it. I might even be willing to go all the way to twenty percent if I get to watch your advisors have an apoplexy when you tell them."

Valentin's grin had a vicious edge and I again caught a glimpse of the calculating Emperor under his pretty exterior. He might not have been groomed for the job from birth, but he seemed to be doing just fine at misleading everyone around him. If everyone underestimated him, that made his job so much easier.

Perhaps I should be taking lessons from him after all.

"I am planning to do a little house cleaning in the coming months," he said. "Having a few advisors spontaneously die off when they find out that the Rogue Queen is teaching me leadership might help speed things along."

"Tired of being stabbed in the back?"

"Yes. And thanks to Commander Adams's loose lips, I finally have enough information to transition some of the worst offenders out without destabilizing the Empire."

"Speaking of Commander Adams," I said, "I heard he escaped. Do you have any information on his location?" He and I were overdue for a little chat.

Valentin scowled. "The coward ran instead of surrendering and saving his troops. We haven't picked up any trace of him yet, but in an escape shuttle it'll take him a while to reach Quint Confederacy space. Maybe the bastard will starve to death on the way."

"One can hope, but roaches tend to be harder to kill than that," I said. I shook off the pleasant thought of Commander Adams's demise and asked, "Where do we go from here?"

"I was serious about us becoming allies," Valentin said. "I would like for us to sign a formal treaty."

"And I was serious when I said my people will never agree," I said. "They want nothing to do with Kos or Quint politically. They came here to escape the war."

"What if the treaty favors the Rogue Coalition?" Valentin asked.

"Maybe," I said doubtfully, "but why would you do that? What do you gain?"

"The treaty is another step toward payment of my debt." He paused, then continued ruefully, "And I'm hoping rumors of the treaty will goad one or more of my advisors into making a mistake."

Before I could respond, someone knocked on Valentin's door. He glanced off screen and his face smoothed into a polite mask. When he looked back at me, he was all Emperor. "We will have to continue this discussion later. Please think about what I said."

I nodded and he cut the link.

———

FOR THE NEXT TWO WEEKS, Valentin and I linked nearly every day, sometimes with vid and sometimes without. We started out with conversations about treaty details, but soon we were discussing a multitude of topics, most of which weren't at all related to treaties or ruling.

Our tentative alliance morphed into true friendship. Beneath the cool Emperor and the charming mask, Valentin was funny and warm and bitingly sarcastic.

We eventually hashed out a treaty agreement that my advisors could get behind. As Queen, I could have unilaterally signed a treaty, but that was a good way to no longer be Queen.

Valentin chose the unilateral route. He seemed to *hope* someone would come after him. Nikolas had apparently gone underground and Valentin wanted to flush him out.

I had negotiated with gusto. I wasn't the Rogue Queen for nothing, newborn friendship notwithstanding, but Valentin had held his own, pushing back against my more outrageous requests and working in a few favorable terms for himself. My respect for him had risen, driving my attraction higher.

Ari and I met in my office to look over the final agreement. I'd already gotten the sign-off from the advisory council, but I wanted one last check to make sure I hadn't missed anything.

As part of the treaty, the Kos Empire agreed not to block trade or hinder Rogue Coalition ships from taking shipping or mercenary jobs. And we could buy their excess food at a discounted price for the next five years.

We had free passage through their territory, but they could not draft us into their war, no matter what happened. If one of their enemies attacked us, Kos had to assist in our defense.

If Quint decided to come after us again, I wanted the assurance of backup with big guns, and I didn't want the Rogue Coalition to get dragged into the war by proxy.

In return, I would give Valentin Kos four weeks of my time for unspecified "intelligence gathering"—his idea of leadership training—and the Rogue Coalition agreed not to go to war with the Kos Empire without provocation. I also agreed to keep my ears open for rumors about kill contracts on Valentin and to share any information pertaining to his advisors' loyalty.

Considering the Kos Empire could squash us like a bug if they put their mind to it, Valentin could've demanded more concessions, but he seemed to be content with the treaty as it was.

Ari finished rereading the agreement. "He's going to sign this, here, in Arx?"

"So he says." He was scheduled to arrive in ten days, and I was trying my very hardest not to let the fluttery feeling in my chest morph into anything more.

Ari's grin took on a sly edge that meant trouble. "Are you excited to see him again?"

There was no point in lying to my best friend—she'd see right through it. "Yes," I said.

"You should give him a chance."

"I don't think he sees me like that," I said. "He wants to be allies."

Ari shot me a highly skeptical look, then sighed.

———

A WEEK before Valentin was scheduled to arrive, Ari asked me to meet her in my private hangar to go over security details. When I arrived, she was waiting for me at the hangar door.

"What's up?" I asked.

"Just wanted to double check a few things," she said. She ushered me through the door into the hangar.

Invictia was over in the main hangar. The shipwrights were working to put her back together again after my firefight with *Deroga*. In her place sat a sleek black ship, a little bigger than *Invictia*. I'd never seen it before.

I turned to Ari, but she had beat a hasty retreat while I wasn't looking. She leaned against the wall next to the door, holding a plasma pistol in a casual grip that I knew could turn deadly in an instant. "Ari?" I asked. She grinned but didn't move.

"What the hell?" I demanded.

"I believe she is standing out of reach of your wrath," Valentin said as he stepped out of the maintenance room beside me.

My hand clutched for a nonexistent weapon as I spun to face him.

Valentin had on black pants and a long-sleeved white shirt that stretched nicely across his sculpted chest. He grinned. "Ari warned me not to startle you if you had a pistol. Since you didn't, I figured it was safe."

Ari snorted and I agreed. Just because I didn't have a pistol didn't mean I was *safe*.

"What are you doing here?" I asked. I told my pulse to settle down and ordered the butterflies out of my stomach. Friends, we were *friends*.

He shrugged. "Vid links are fine, but I wanted to see you. I found myself nowhere near this sector, so I decided to stop by," he said with a sheepish grin. "Ari helped me get in. Surprise!"

I smiled at him. I had to admit, I was glad to see him in person, too. "Is this your ship parked in my hangar?"

"Yes. *Korax* is my personal ship."

I looked away from him and back to the ship. "She's a beauty," I said.

"Yes, she is," he agreed softly.

His words swept over me, and I wondered if he meant them the way they sounded. I darted a glance at him, but his expression didn't give anything away.

"How long are you staying?" I asked.

"I have to head back early tomorrow morning," he said. "Something came up and I can't make the trip next week, but I wanted to see you and sign the treaty, so I snuck away for the day."

"How many guards did you bring? Do I have to worry about them skulking around invisible?"

"Luka, you heard the lady. Stop skulking," Valentin said.

Nothing happened.

"Now, Luka," Valentin commanded. An armed soldier in combat armor blinked into view next to the ship's cargo ramp. "Samara, meet Luka Fox, my bodyguard. Luka, meet Queen Samara Rani and her head of security, Arietta Mueller."

"You didn't think combat armor was a *little much*?" I asked Valentin drily.

Valentin heaved a long-suffering sigh. "Luka has heard about you and he's paranoid about my safety."

"He loses the armor, or he stays with the ship," I said.

"Agreed," Valentin said. He glanced at his bodyguard. Luka scowled and stripped out of his armor with brisk efficiency.

Valentin turned me around to face him, then brushed gentle fingers over what I knew were dark circles under my eyes. My thoughts derailed.

"How are you?" he asked quietly.

"I'm completely healed," I said. "Just busy."

Now that we had food again, people had seemingly lost their damn minds. I knew they were just blowing off steam after months of focused good behavior, but cracking skulls and dishing out punishments had kept me busy enough that exhaustion plagued my steps.

"Let's get this treaty signed so you have one less thing to deal with."

I nodded. It *would* be nice not to have to think about it anymore, but I'd gotten used to our daily conversations. I would miss them.

Luka stalked toward us wearing black pants and a long-sleeved black shirt. As he approached, I noticed he was big, taller than Valentin, and all muscle.

He had a shock of wavy, ice blond hair that looked like it'd spent too much time in his helmet, then he'd run his hands through it and called it good. His fierce scowl might be classified a weapon, but I also counted at least three other concealed guns on him.

"Expecting a war?" I asked.

His scowl deepened.

Okay, then. "You're here as a guest. You will respect our laws. Understand?"

Luka nodded once.

"Welcome to Arx," I said.

We passed Ari on the way out. I smiled at her and flicked my eyes back toward the ship. Her expression turned angelic. Luka demanded Ari exit first, but she just grinned at him and planted herself more firmly against the wall. When Valentin and I continued out of the hangar, Luka was forced to leave Ari and follow.

I had no doubt that by the time Ari left the hangar, the Rogue Coalition would be the proud new owner of an undamaged set of Kos special-ops combat armor.

———

BECAUSE WE DEPENDED on jobs from the Kos Empire, people were cool but civil to Valentin. We signed the treaty in front of my advisory council, then escaped to spend time catching up in person. We had dinner that included real food and stayed up late talking. Even so, the minutes slipped away all too quickly.

At some point I must've nodded off because the next thing I knew, Valentin was shaking me awake.

"Sorry to wake you so early," he said softly, "but I have to leave."

I blinked and sat up. We were on the couch in the living room of the guest suite. Someone had put a blanket over me and I'd been using his shoulder as a pillow. Heat rushed into my cheeks.

"You should've woke me earlier," I said. "I would've left so you could go to bed."

"I don't mind," he said. "I fell asleep right after you."

I stood and stretched. When Valentin was ready, I escorted him and Luka back to my private hangar. Luka scowled at the empty spot where he'd discarded his armor.

"I believe you have something of mine, Queen Rani," he said. His voice was a pleasant rumble, even with irritation lacing the words.

I gave him my most guileless smile. "What do you mean?" I asked politely. "Did you forget something in the guest suite?"

Valentin burst into rueful laughter. "I told you the armor was a bad idea, Luka. Please get the ship ready for takeoff. *Now*," Valentin clarified.

Luka disappeared into the ship after one last grumpy scowl. I tossed him a jaunty wave in return.

Valentin stepped close and my heart rate picked up. "When will my leadership training begin?" he asked.

"Soon," I promised.

I had a few things to wrap up in Arx, and then I had a stop to make. After that, I planned to head to Koan for the first of the four weeks I owed Valentin. I figured I'd help him gather intel on his advisors, but I wasn't entirely sure what *he* expected.

Satisfaction filled Valentin's expression and his gray eyes gleamed like molten metal. "Good," he said. He stepped back and offered me his hand with a shallow bow. I clasped his hand, but rather than giving me a handshake, he lifted my hand to his mouth and pressed his warm lips to the back of it. Tingles raced up my arm.

He straightened but kept my hand. "I would've paid you ten million," he confessed with a grin.

"I would've accepted five," I countered without missing a beat.

He laughed and pulled me closer, until my chest brushed his. I had to tilt my head back to hold his gaze. "Don't wait too long," he murmured, his expression oddly intent.

He paused for a moment, then dipped his head and brushed his lips against mine. My eyes slid closed and desire licked down my spine. I arched into him and nibbled his bottom lip.

His mouth opened and his tongue slid against mine. I shivered at the sensation. Valentin's kiss was leisurely, a slow exploration, but I could feel how tightly he held himself. I licked into his mouth and he groaned before pulling away.

"Come to Koan *soon*," he demanded.

I nodded my agreement, stunned by the kiss.

Valentin stepped back, but his eyes blazed with desire and his hands dropped reluctantly from my shoulders. "Farewell, Queen Rani, until we meet again," he said formally.

"Farewell, Emperor Kos. I will see you soon."

He bowed again and then took his leave.

I pressed my fingers to my lips and watched until his ship disappeared into the gray sky.

EPILOGUE

C old rain sluiced over my tattered raincoat as I stumbled through the darkened city. The few people still out in the terrible weather took one look at my shabby attire, empty right sleeve, and listing gait and moved out of my way.

I shambled slowly, stopping frequently to lean against the expensive buildings lining the wide sidewalk. More than one doorman braved the storm to shoo me on my way. Their tenants didn't want riffraff hanging about, sullying up the place.

I shuffled to the next block. I'd only gone a few meters when a sleek black transport stopped in the middle of the block next to a brightly lit, awning-covered building entrance.

A large, heavily muscled man stepped out of the car. I watched him out of the corner of my eye. He stared hard at me, but I kept my face buried in my scarf and my walk wobbly. After a few seconds, he nodded to the second man in the car and another hulking guard appeared.

The second guard at least remembered to step between me and the transport door. A slender third man emerged. I only caught glimpses of him, but it was enough to confirm he was my target. The little group hustled toward the entrance.

One step.

Two.

The transport slid away.

I drew my electroshock pistol with my concealed right arm and shot the both of the guards with stun rounds. Jax froze for half a second as his guards fell, then he lunged for the door.

He didn't make it.

I shot him twice for good measure, then dropped the drunken act and hurried to collect him. I had maybe thirty seconds before unwanted company showed up. Sniping him from the building across the street would've been cleaner, but I wanted to question him about what he'd told Quint first, and that required close quarters.

An unremarkable man in his late thirties, with wavy brown hair just starting to gray at the temples, Jackson Leopold Russell looked like a middle manager at a bank. You would never guess from his appearance that he was one of the foremost hackers in the universe.

I leaned down and peered into his terrified eyes, then pressed the injector of sedative to his neck and pulled the trigger. "You forgot one very important thing," I whispered with a lethal smile, "Quint may have paid better, but I *always* keep my promises."

SNEAK PEEK AT POLARIS RISING

The steel toe of my boot slammed into the blond merc's knee with a satisfying crunch. He went down with a curse, but the two men holding my arms didn't release me, even as I struggled in their grasp. The blow had been more luck than skill, but it was enough to make the fourth mercenary pause before trying to grab my legs again.

I planted my feet and pushed back as hard as I could. The men behind me barely budged. I was a decently strong woman, but they each outweighed me by fifty or more pounds and the physics just weren't on my side. My self-defense tutor had warned me that one day I would regret slacking off in lessons—turns out, she was right.

"Stop fighting, you little bitch, or I'll stun you again," the blond warned. He climbed to his feet and waved his stunstick as if I needed a visual reminder. He wasn't the ship's captain, so he must be the mercenary commander. He was young for commander, but mercs weren't known to have long lives.

The ship's captain stood back while the merc crew tried to wrestle me farther into the ship. The skin around his left eye was fiercely red. He'd have a shiner by tomorrow, thanks to me. That blow had been more skill than luck, but not enough to save me.

The captain was a handsome man, older, with gray at the temples of his dark hair. He looked like a gentleman, not a bounty hunter, and that had allowed him to get close enough to grab me. The rest of his crew was standard-issue mercenary: big, mean, and calculating. As soon as I'd caught sight of them, I'd known that I'd made a mistake.

I hoped it wouldn't be my last.

I fought on, determined. As long as the ship was still docked, I had a chance. I could escape and disappear into the crowds of the space station until I could find another ship. I was good at hiding.

The blond lost his patience. Before I could kick him away, he hit me with the stunstick. I screamed as my body lit up in agony. The mercs dropped me. My head hit the metal deck and pain blazed bright before dulling to a low throb. The world went dark and floaty.

"John, what are you doing? Don't hurt her!" the captain shouted. "If she shows up with so much as a bruise, von Hasenberg will kill the lot of us."

"Where do ya want her?" one of the other men asked.

"She can stay in my—" the captain started, but the blond, presumably John, cut him off.

"Put her in with Loch. That'll teach the little hellion a lesson. It's not like he's using the space anyway."

The crew laughed uneasily. Whoever Loch was, he made them nervous, and it took a lot to rattle a merc crew. Yay for me.

I tried to struggle as they picked me up by my arms and legs, but my muscles weren't responding, thanks to the blow to the head. And the nanobots in my blood that should be repairing any tissue damage were also susceptible to the stunstick. They'd recover in a few minutes, but until then I had to wait for natural healing.

Nanobots, or nanos, were available to anyone who could

afford the exorbitant price tag. I'd been injected with them as a newborn.

A door squeaked open and the men cursed quietly as they tried to maneuver me through the opening.

"Put her on the bed," the captain said. "Carefully."

"Why, Gerald, you shouldn't have," a deep voice rumbled from within the room.

"I didn't," the captain snapped. "She's worth three times what you are, Loch, so you don't want to make me choose which of you to keep," he continued. "Keep your comments to yourself or I'll purge you. Same thing happens if you even look at her sideways."

One of the men grumbled something too low to catch.

"She give you that eye?" Loch asked. "Did you try to get some on the side and she took offense?"

"Stun him," the captain said flatly.

The electric hiss of a stunstick was followed by a grunt. I'd never heard anyone get stunned without screaming; it didn't seem possible.

I cracked my eyes open a tiny bit. The light panel on the ceiling glowed softly. Were there supposed to be two of them?

"She's coming to," one of the men warned.

I squinted, trying to get my vision to clear, and when that didn't work, I closed my eyes and willed the nanos to work faster. They weren't affected by my desire for speed, sadly, so I resigned myself to wait.

"Everyone out. Pull up the separator and leave it up. Let's see how the little princess likes her new palace," John said.

The faint ozone smell of an active energy field reached my nose. Booted footsteps exited the room, then the door creaked closed and locked with a metallic *thunk*.

I wiggled my fingers and toes. It was a start.

"You alive?" Loch asked.

Mostly, I slurred. "They stunned me then dropped me head-first onto the deck. I'll live."

"Where are we?"

"Station orbiting Theta Sagittarii Dwarf One," I said. I sat up and closed my eyes against the light-headedness. In addition to my throbbing head, I was sore from being hit with a stunstick twice in an hour. Overall, it could've been worse, but not by much.

"Damn," he muttered. I was with him there. I didn't know why he was concerned, but I knew that we were just two short jumps away from the gate that would deliver us directly to Earth. That only gave me a little over a week—in open space no less—to escape.

I cracked my eyes open. I sat on a narrow cot with a thin mattress and no sheets or blankets. A quick glance confirmed I was in a standard holding cell on a Yamado frigate—only the Yamados etched their House symbol, a crane, on every door.

Far more interesting than the Yamado door was the man sharing the cell with me. Even through the slight distortion of the blue energy barrier, I saw that deeply bronzed flesh wrapped his heavily muscled frame. Broad shoulders tapered to a narrow waist with rippling abs. Defined arms and muscled legs completed the picture.

It was only after I'd stared for a solid five seconds that I realized why I was seeing quite so much of him: he had been stripped down to only a skintight pair of black boxer briefs.

I jerked my gaze up to his face and blinked in surprise when I met luminescent eyes. But when I met his eyes a second time, they were brown. Ocular augments existed, but as far as I knew, they permanently altered your eyes. It could've been a trick of the light, but it was worth watching.

His gaze was sharp and direct. Several weeks' worth of dark beard shadowed his jaw. His hair was the same length and I wondered if he normally kept his head shaved. The scruffiness made it hard to tell his exact age, but he was probably a few years older than my twenty-three.

"Like what you see?" he asked with a smirk.

"Yes," I said after a few more seconds of frank appraisal. Surprise flashed across his face, but why would I lie? He was beautifully built. He was perhaps not conventionally handsome but he had a deep, primal appeal. One glance and you knew that this was a man who could take care of problems. Add that deep, gravelly voice and he was temptation incarnate.

Now that I wasn't mesmerized by the amount of flesh on display, I saw that he was chained to the wall behind him from both ankles and wrists. The chains disappeared into the wall and their length could be adjusted. Right now, they were short enough that he couldn't sit comfortably. Whoever he was, the mercs weren't taking any chances with him.

I stood and wavered as sore muscles protested. Damn stunsticks to hell. With the bed taking up more than half of the floor space, there was barely any room to walk. I knew from the schematics that the cell was a meter and a half wide by three meters long. The barrier dropped down just past the two-meter mark, leaving my unfortunate cellmate trapped in a one-and-a-half by one-meter box. He wouldn't be able to lie flat even if they released the chains enough to let him.

The barrier was blue, which should mean safe, but I'd known some people who thought it was funny to reprogram the system. I carefully reached out a finger and pressed it against the field. I didn't get shocked, so I wouldn't have to worry about avoiding it. Today was finally looking up.

"What are you doing?" Loch asked.

"Exploring."

He raised a skeptical eyebrow but didn't say anything else.

In addition to the bed, the only other features of the room were a tiny sink and, on the other side of the barrier, a toilet. The cell wasn't designed to be permanently divided the way the mercs were using it. The barrier was meant to hold the prisoner away from the door while the cell was cleaned or maintained.

"Do you know how many crew are on board?" I asked.

"At least eight, maybe nine."

A merchant ship of this size could be efficiently managed by as few as six, but the standard crew size was between eight and ten. If it was loaded out for maximum crew space, they could have up to fourteen.

The lights flickered and the floor vibrated with the subtle hum of running engines. The captain wasn't wasting any time getting under way. I moved around the room, touching the cool steel walls seemingly at random. I knew we were being watched, and I didn't want to make our audience nervous just yet.

"First time in a cell?"

"It's rather small," I said.

Loch barked out a laugh. "You get used to it. Let me guess, you're a surfacer."

Surfacers were people who grew up primarily on planets. Every day they woke up to big blue—or green or pink—skies, lots of solid ground under their feet, and plenty of room to roam.

Spacers, the people who grew up in the ships and stations floating around and between those same planets, seemed to think that surfacers had it easier. Even I knew that wasn't always the case.

"What gave me away?" I asked. I'd lived entirely on ships and stations for the last two years. I'd gotten used to the smaller spaces, but I still longed for the wide-open blue sky of my home.

His answer was interrupted by a male voice through the intercom speaker. "Stand away from the door."

I had not expected anyone so soon and this cell didn't give me much room to fight. Chains rattled behind me. I glanced back as Loch stood to his full height. At a meter eighty in boots, I was a tall woman. Loch still had me beat by at least ten centimeters. Damn. Why were the attractive ones always criminals?

The door swung inward to reveal a young man with a shaggy mop of blond hair that looked like it had never seen a brush. He held an armful of frilly fuchsia fabric and a stunstick. "Give me any trouble and I've got permission to zap you," he warned.

"Give *me* any trouble, and you'll get a boot to the teeth," I replied. "No permission required."

He almost smiled. What do you know, a merc with a sense of humor—it was like I'd found a unicorn. I'd have to blame it on his age because he looked all of sixteen.

"You're having dinner with the captain," he said. "Here's your dress." He dropped the frilly monstrosity on the bed.

"No," I said. I didn't balk because of the frills, which were horrible, or the color, which was equally horrible. I refused because it was a dress. I had no problem with dresses in general, but on a ship full of hostile men, it was smarter for everyone if I didn't go out of my way to advertise the fact that I was female.

"Umm, no to which part?" he asked hesitantly.

"I'll dine with the captain, but I'm wearing my own clothes." I had on a sturdy pair of black cargo pants, heavy black boots, and a long-sleeved black shirt. I wasn't trying to win *Monochromatic Monthly*'s best dressed award, but black was easy to find, easy to match, and generally didn't show dirt or grease stains as fast as other colors. Win, win, win.

"Uhh…"

I tilted my head ever so slightly and let my expression frost over. "I will dine with the captain, but I *will* be wearing my own clothes."

He ducked his head. "Yes, ma'am," he said. "Right this way."

A deep chuckle followed us out.

———

The kid gripped the stunstick like he expected me to jump him at any moment. I guess word of my arrival had already spread to the rest of the crew. And, honestly, if they'd sent anyone else, I probably would've made an attempt at escape. If it came down to it, I would go through the kid if he stood between me and freedom, but it wouldn't be my first choice.

As we walked, I took in my surroundings. The captain had not spent much on interior upgrades. The walls were flat gray metal, the floor was steel grating, and the lights were few and far between. I saw at least three major wiring issues that would get them grounded if a safety officer ever bothered to do an inspection. The ship was holding up well for her age, but it was apparent that either the captain or his crew didn't truly love her.

I, however, saw plenty to love. Access panels were open or missing. The wiring issues would be an easy way to disable some key ship systems. And the layout matched the reference layout, so I could find my way around even in the dark.

The kid led me to the captain's chambers, which were exactly where I expected them to be. Yamado had been making this style ship for approximately a thousand years, give or take a few, and I was suddenly very glad that they liked to stick to tradition.

The captain's entertaining space was brightly lit, with real wood floors, thick rugs, and antique furniture. A table that could seat sixteen dominated the middle of the room. Two place settings were laid out on the right side. The captain sat in an overstuffed chair next to a sideboard that was being used as a liquor cabinet. He rose to meet me. The skin around his left eye was already darkening.

I pulled on my public persona, affixed my politest smile to my lips, and tried not to think stabby thoughts. "Thank you for the dinner invitation, Captain."

"Of course, my dear, of course," he said. "Ada, may I call you Ada?" He continued before I had a chance to respond, "I know we got off to a bad start, but now that we are under way, I thought we could put all of that behind us. I know your father is quite eager to have you home."

"I'm sure he is," I murmured. Albrecht von Hasenberg was nothing if not thorough. When his security team couldn't find me and drag me back for my engagement party, he went above and beyond by posting an enormous bounty for my safe return. Of course, he told the news, he was devastated that I was "missing." He failed to mention that I had left of my own volition. Or that I'd been gone for two years.

"Can I get you some wine? Or perhaps brandy?" the captain asked.

"Wine would be lovely, thank you," I said. I knew where this road led. I'd been playing this game since I could talk. The captain wanted something, and he thought—rightly—that House von Hasenberg could help him get it. As patriarch of one of the three High Houses, very few people in the universe wielded more power than my father.

As the fifth of six children, I wielded no power in House von Hasenberg at all. But the good captain didn't know that, and outside of the Consortium, my name carried its own power.

"Captain—"

"Please, call me Gerald," he interrupted as he handed me a glass of wine with a shallow bow, "Gerald Pearson, at your service."

I let a chill creep into my expression and he flushed. You did not interrupt a member of a High House if you wanted to keep breathing. By acknowledging who my father was, he'd moved me from *bounty* to *potential ally*, and now I was quickly moving to *superior*. It was his first mistake, but I didn't hold it against him. He'd never had to swim with the glittering sharks of the Consortium. I had, and I excelled at it.

I hated it, but I excelled at it.

"Gerald," I said with a dismissive little sniff, "have you already sent word to my father that I was found?"

"Of course, my lady," he said, practically tripping over himself to get back into my good graces. "I let him know as soon as I returned to the ship. I also sent along a copy of our flight plan."

Damn. Interstellar communication could be slow, but we were close enough to the gate that the message had probably already made it through. I would not put it past my father to send a fleet escort to meet us at the gate. My escape time just dropped to three or four days.

I sized the captain up as I toyed with my wineglass and made polite small talk. He was not a merc who had worked his way up to captain. He didn't have the hardness, the craftiness that mercenaries wore like second skins. A true merc commander would never be so easy to play.

"Shall we dine?" he asked.

"Yes, thank you," I said.

I made sure his wineglass was kept topped off and waited until the second course had been cleared away. "How can I help you, Gerald?" I asked in my warmest tone.

It took two more courses, but eventually the story came out. He was a merchant fallen on hard times, but he still had a ship. He'd partnered with the bounty hunters specifically to hunt Loch. They'd found him a few days ago, but Loch had killed two men during his capture, including the previous commander.

The mercenaries didn't respect Gerald and he was afraid they were plotting his demise. And he was just so lucky to have found me because his third cousin once removed was married to a von Hasenberg second cousin's sister-in-law and he just knew he had a great deal he could contribute to the House, considering he was almost family.

I nodded along and made all the right encouraging noises. The picture became clear. Even if I managed to overpower Gerald and take him hostage, the mercs wouldn't care. He'd already created the flight plan, so the ship would deliver us to Earth without any further input from him. It was time to end the evening.

"I should go," I said.

"You should stay," he slurred. "You can sleep in my room." He staggered to his feet.

I considered it. He was drunk enough that he'd probably be

asleep as soon as he hit the bed. But I needed time to devise an escape plan and I couldn't be caught wandering around the ship. So I just had to make sure this wasn't my last dinner with the captain. I stood as well.

"Gerald, you naughty man," I laughed and lightly touched his arm. "I never sleep with a man on the first date."

He flushed and spluttered. "I didn't mean—"

The tone of the engine changed and my stomach dropped as the FTL drive engaged. We'd traveled far enough away from the station for our first jump. The lights flickered as the ship switched to auxiliary power. The hum of the engines ratcheted up and then went silent. Less than a minute later, my stomach settled and the main engines started up again. Depending on the age of the ship, it would take up to a week to recharge the FTL drive for the next jump. I had to be gone before that time was up.

"I will see you tomorrow for dinner, yes?" I asked with a coy smile.

"Yes, yes, of course, my lady. The lad'll see you back to your quarte—" He flinched. "I'm terribly sorry for your accommodations, but I'm afraid the mercs won't like it if I move you."

"It is fine. I like it; it makes me feel safe." And I was surprised to find that it was true.

———

The same kid from before was waiting for me outside of the captain's door. I wondered if he stood there all the time, and if so, was he looking out for the captain's interests or the mercenaries'?

"What's your name?" I asked.

"Charles, but everyone calls me Chuck."

"Chuck, I'm Ada. Pleased to meet you." He ducked his head but didn't respond.

We returned to my cell by the same path we'd taken earlier. When we arrived, the display next to the door showed Loch still standing in the back section. He had to have been standing for hours, but he wasn't slumped or fidgeting. I made a quick decision that I hoped I wouldn't come to regret.

"The captain said to lower the barrier," I said. "So that if I need to use the facilities, they are available."

"Umm..." Chuck stole a glance at the control screen, but he clearly had no idea what to do.

I swept past him. "Allow me."

"I don't think—"

But I was already tapping on the screen. I lowered the separator, set the lights to stay on all night at a dim setting, and lengthened Loch's chains. He wouldn't be able to stretch out, but at least he could sit. And I would remain out of his reach.

"Easy peasy," I said. "I could teach you, if you'd like."

The kid eyed the video display with distrust, but it was easy to see that Loch remained chained. I prayed that Loch wouldn't move and give away the fact that his chains were longer, but he still stood in the same position. I wondered if he was sleeping standing up. Was that even possible?

"I don't need help from you," Chuck said. "The crew is teaching me everything I need to know." He swung the door open. "Now get in there and don't give me any trouble."

I entered the dim cell and the door slammed closed behind me. Without the energy field separating us, Loch seemed bigger, more immediate, and vastly more dangerous. *The enemy of my enemy is my friend.* I just had to keep reminding myself that we both wanted the same thing.

I tilted my head slightly toward the door, and Loch barely shook his head. I hadn't heard the kid leave, either, so I had to assume we had an audience.

"Did you miss me while I was gone?" I asked.

"No."

"Ah, that's too bad. Would you like to hear about the captain's quarters?"

"No."

I couldn't help the slightly evil edge to my smile as I began to describe, in excruciating detail, the captain's dining room. Every rug was lovingly described, as was every vase, flower, piece of furniture, and place setting.

After five minutes, Loch stepped away from the wall with a rattle of chains. "He's gone, but feel free to keep talking. I was nearly asleep."

"Did they feed you?" I asked.

He shrugged. "I ate."

I'd spent three months as part of a merc crew shortly after I left home. I'd been on my own for the first time and thought—incorrectly—that being part of a crew would help my homesickness. It wasn't a total waste, though, because I learned a great many lessons in that short time and the nomadic lifestyle helped me stay ahead of Father's security team in the crucial first months.

One of the lessons I learned was that bounty-hunting mercenaries, by and large, were ruthless and sadistic. Even the higher-tier crew I joined was not exempt. They loved to torture their captives by providing just enough food to prevent the captive from dying, but not enough to prevent constant, aching hunger. It also kept the captive weak enough to be easy to manage, so in their minds, it was a win-win.

Loch did not look weak, but according to the captain they'd only had him for a few days.

I pulled two dinner rolls wrapped in a paper napkin out of one of the pockets on my pants. After all, what was the point of pants with so many pockets if I wasn't going to use them? And if they failed to pat me down after dinner, then that was hardly my fault.

"Sadly, nothing else would transport well, so it is bread or nothing. But I'm willing to give you these two delicious rolls in exchange for your name. I know the mercs call you Loch, but I don't know if that's your first or last name or something they made up."

"You're trying to bribe me with bread?"

"Yes. Is it working? I'm Ada."

"I know who you are," Loch said.

It was my turn to be surprised. I might be a von Hasenberg, but I'd never been in the spotlight like my four eldest siblings. Those four all looked like younger versions of our father, even poor Hannah and Bianca. I had the golden skin, dark hair, and blue-gray eyes of our mother. Only our youngest sister, Catarina, shared my coloring.

"And so you are...?" I prompted.

"Marcus Loch," he finally replied.

"Pleased to meet you," I said. I tossed him the bread, napkin and all. We might be making polite conversation, but I had no doubt that Mr. Marcus Loch would eat me alive if I ventured too close.

Marcus Loch. The name sounded familiar. I mentally sorted through the rosters of important people in all three High Houses, trying to place him. I knew he wasn't part of House von Hasenberg. He couldn't be directly part of House Yamado or House Rockhurst, either, because he would have their name. So either he was a distant relation or an in-law, but I couldn't remember. Where had I heard that name and who had he pissed off to get such a bounty?

"Let me save you some time," he said as if reading my mind. "I'm Marcus Loch, the so-called Devil of Fornax Zero, and the man with the highest bounty in the 'verse... at least until you showed up."

It was only thanks to long practice that I managed to keep my expression perfectly placid. Now the chains made sense, as did the mercs' wariness. The Royal Consortium claimed that Marcus Loch had killed at least a dozen of his commanding officers and fellow soldiers during the suppression of the Fornax Rebellion. Then he disappeared.

The Consortium put out an ever-increasing bounty, but so far no bounty hunter had been able to bring him in to claim it. Rumor had it that he'd been caught six or seven times, but every time he had escaped and left nothing but a pile of bodies behind.

Marcus Loch was a deserter, a killer, and a traitor to the Consortium. And he was just the man I needed.

———

Preorder Polaris Rising today!

ABOUT THE AUTHOR

Jessie Mihalik has a degree in Computer Science and a love of all things geeky. A software engineer by trade, Jessie now writes full time from her home in Texas. When she's not writing, she can be found playing co-op video games with her husband, trying out new board games, or reading books pulled from her overflowing bookshelves.

CONNECT WITH JESSIE:

www.jessiemihalik.com
Twitter: @jessiemihalik
Facebook: www.facebook.com/JessMihalik
Want all of the latest book news, info, and snippets delivered straight to your inbox? Sign up for Jessie's newsletter!